Welcome to Spicetown

A Spicetown Mystery

Sheri Richey

Copyright © 2019 Sheri S. Richey. All rights reserved. No part of this book may be reproduced or transmitted in any form or by any means, electronic or mechanical, including photocopying, recording or by an information storage or retrieval system now known or hereto after invented—except by a reviewer who may quote brief passages in a review to be printed in a magazine or newspaper—without permission in writing from the publisher.

For further information, contact the publisher: Amazon Publishing.

The author assumes no responsibility for errors or omissions that are inadvertent or inaccurate. This is a work of fiction and is not intended to reflect actual events or persons.

ISBN: 9781795303538

Cover art by Mariah Sinclair
Editing by Celtic Frog Editing

Chapter One

With another year behind her, Cora Mae Bingham logged off her computer and sat back in her chair with a sigh on her lips as the screen display changed to a peaceful ocean view. At the end of her tenth year as mayor of Spicetown, it was time to make plans for the future.

She brushed crumbs from her lap, residuals from a holiday cookie she had snacked on earlier, after making the silent vow of millions that she would be healthier and thinner in the coming year.

She always enjoyed a fresh new year, but tonight she was feeling weary. Having city hall closed for the holidays should have been restful, but instead she found that taking time to relax made it more difficult when it was time to return to work. If she let herself step out of those daily habits, she truly saw how taxing they were.

The holidays were stressful and dragged her back to memories of younger days before she carried so much responsibility for the citizens of Spicetown. A new year felt like a clean slate. With a rest over New Year's Day, she'd be ready to start fresh.

"Mayor?" Amanda Morgan, Cora's assistant, stuck her head around the edge of the door with an apologetic wrinkle in her forehead. "I know you're ready to leave, but Mr. Salzman is out in the lobby and he's asking to see you."

"I guess the year wasn't meant to be over yet," Cora said mostly to herself as she sighed again and leaned back in her chair. "That's okay, Amanda. You can send him in."

Cora opened her lower desk drawer and pulled out her large satchel purse as Harvey Salzman walked through her door.

"What's up, Saucy? I've had a long day and I'm ready to call it a year." Proclaiming the end of the year gave her a silent pleasure.

"I know it's late and I apologize Mayor, but this couldn't wait until next year."

Harvey Salzman, Saucy to his friends, sat down in the chair across from Cora. With his hands resting on his kneecaps, he bounced the heel of one foot nervously. He was a thin, lanky, but energetic senior citizen, passionate about his community. Cora Mae imagined he recorded every incident of littering and jaywalking that occurred in Spicetown. Anxiety shimmered around him like a neon glow.

"I'm not gone yet, so let's wrap this year up. How can I help you?"

"Well, somebody stole the stop sign at the end of Dill Seed Drive and that's a dangerous corner to not have a stop sign. It can't wait until next year. There might be a wreck, especially tonight with it being New Year's Eve. You know there will be intoxicated people around and they might just drive right into my house in the middle of the night! How can I ever go to sleep for the worry? It was probably those kids I told you about. They are up to no good. Loitering around, looking for trouble—"

"Did you report the theft to the police?" Cora interrupted before Saucy could recycle the story and pulled off her reading glasses to let her neck chain catch them.

"Oh, yes ma'am," Saucy said with an exaggerated shake of his head. "Chief Connie sent me right over here to catch you before you left for the night, so you could replace that sign."

Cora stifled a smile. She had to give Chief Conrad Harris a point for that move. She had been prepared to do the same thing to him, but Connie beat her to it.

"Ok, Saucy. I'll take care of it." Cora rose from her chair and put her bag on her shoulder. She peeked out of the window between the large metal venetian blinds at Ole' Thyme Italian Restaurant across the street. It had been dark outside for almost an hour already and the crowd at the restaurant was picking up. Cora wouldn't be getting dinner there tonight.

"I certainly hope so, Mayor. I have to get my sleep and I know I won't get a wink until this problem is corrected. You know I appreciate everything you do for this town."

"Happy New Year, Saucy. I need to get home now." Cora held out her arm to usher Harvey Salzman through her door and noticed Amanda had already made her escape. Saucy continued to reiterate the same point as if his thoughts ran on a hamster wheel until Cora made her way down the back hallway to the employee parking in the back of the building, leaving Saucy to exit through the front lobby.

Before walking out the back door, she stopped and peered into Jimmy Kole's office. Jimmy was in charge of Spicetown Streets and Alleys and his day had lasted even longer than hers.

"Hey, Jimmy. Do you have anybody still out at the shed?" Cora hoped there were still city employees on the clock, so she could get the stop sign hung without an act of Congress.

"Yeah, there are two guys still out there gassing up the trucks. You need something?"

"I do. Would you please call out there and tell them to go hang a stop sign at Dill Seed Drive and Sage Street? Somebody stole it and Saucy is up a tree about it."

"Does it have to be done tonight? It's already dark."

"Do you want me to give Saucy your home address?" Cora laughed as incredulity spread across Jimmy's face.

"I'm on it." Jimmy lifted the phone receiver to his ear with a grin showing off the dimple in his left cheek.

"I knew I could count on you." Cora left through the back door with a small smile on her lips as she buttoned up her coat. That was the closure she needed to finish the year out.

§

Conrad Harris poured water in the back of the coffeemaker in his office and studied it until he heard it trickle. He yearned for the warm scent to wrap around him even if he rarely got a chance to drink it.

The rest of the Spicetown Police force drank coffee in the dispatch room. Ordering everyone not to touch the Chief's coffee had worked out well for him. He added a touch of cinnamon and a vanilla creamer to make it everyone's envy. There were few joys in his daily life and this was one of them.

He was certain he would need the coffee as he expected a late night. New Year's Eve meant multiple noise complaints, but he couldn't ignore the raw wariness that niggled inside him. He had learned over the years to give this his full attention.

On the surface, it shouldn't be a difficult night since the city wasn't staging an event or doing any New Year's Eve display. The new sheriff had decided to hold a county firework display and discouraged the cities in the county from competing with him.

Conrad hadn't voted for this new sheriff, and he suspected the new sheriff probably realized that. Bobby Bell was not a stranger to Conrad. He had known him for years when they had worked together as police officers in the city. Bobby made reckless choices and his ego seemed to do his thinking for him.

Conrad wasn't disappointed the mayor had taken the hint and advertised the county fireworks plan to the citizens of Spicetown rather than initiate any display herself. He supposed she did it to save money, but he knew from experience that it would have been a lot of extra work for him. It was trouble he didn't need.

"Hey, Chief," Officer Hobson said as he came in the side door and down the hall past Conrad's office.

"Wink," Conrad called out as he saw him walk by. "Stop by on your way back out."

"Sure thing, Chief."

Wink, Conrad's unofficial right-hand man, had one eye that didn't open more than half way. He always told everyone that it was his good eye and no one ever knew if he was joking or not.

Conrad poured his fresh coffee, breathing in deeply over the cup until the healing warmth floated over him and waited for Wink to return. Maybe it was time to try again to get the City

Council to consider promoting him to lieutenant. Sadly, Wink did the work without the title or pay.

"Hey, Chief," Wink said as he returned to perch his tall lanky frame against the edge of the door to Conrad's office with a travel cup of coffee in his hand.

"Wink, have you been through the intersection of Dill Seed and Sage Street? The stop sign was down earlier and I didn't know if the city got a new one up yet or not."

"I haven't been that way, but I'll check while I'm out and let you know. Saucy must have been off his watch." Wink grinned as he turned for the side door.

"Everybody has to sleep sometime."

Conrad wondered when he would get that chance. He sipped his coffee and tried to remember the last good sleep he'd had. So much for small town chief being a relaxing job. If he had something or someone waiting for him to retire, he might not have stayed for thirteen years. *Here I am, still married to the job.*

Sheri Richey

Chapter Two

    Cora slipped off her shoes and sat back in her favorite chair. She tossed the chenille throw over her legs and put her feet up in relief. With her cheese and crackers arranged on a plate, she stirred her tea to watch it tunnel deeply in the center.

    The fatigue was deep, but she wasn't sleepy. Her mind was sharply spinning out the day's events to make room for her plans for next year. She lifted her favorite mug and let the rising heat warm the tip of her nose. This was her favorite moment of the day. She was content to sit in silence with nothing to interrupt her thoughts and marvel at how wonderful the lack of sound could be.

    There had been staff shortages that day. Those that had worked had been debating whether field peas or northern beans were required to bring good luck in the future year and who would win the football games. Cora was just thankful for a day the city hall would be closed. She planned to sit right there in her comfortable chair with her cat rubbing against her calves until she had to return to work.

She expected her plans for next year to meet staunch resistance, but they would bring needed change to Spicetown. There were several things that needed improvement, and she had ignored them long enough. This might be her last term and her last chance to make a difference. She would have to be strong to get through it.

She wanted to get the local library connected to the interstate library exchange and form a citizen's group to support the animal shelter. She wanted to fix up the old popcorn factory building the city had taken ownership of, so it could be used for banquets and meetings. She wanted to have the flowers in the planters around the main street replaced with the spices their climate would tolerate and plaques posted identifying each plant. She wanted Spicetown listed in the state travel directory and knew she would have to work with the Chamber of Commerce President Miriam Landry to get that done even though that would be a personal struggle. She needed sidewalks repaired, the annual water test order, the website updated, and the sewer pipe on Allspice Avenue replaced.

If it was the last thing she did, she wanted the statue of John Spicer erected on Paprika Parkway before she retired. John Spicer was the man her town was named after and she wanted that known to visitors. People coming through Spicetown and seeing all the street names and businesses left thinking that Spicetown grew spices when that was not the case at all. Although she promoted the uniqueness of the town's flavor, she wanted people to understand it was not the origins of the town name.

She had so many plans, each competing with the other for her time and attention, that she constantly re-prioritized them when battling for the funds to implement them. This year she was going to accomplish something, not just keep the town running as she had been.

When her thoughts drifted back to the debate of northern beans or field peas, she gave up on sleep and got up to get her notebook. She needed to visualize concrete plans and make her own good luck for the next year.

§

Conrad finished his Styrofoam-plated dinner from the Ole' Thyme Italian Restaurant and brushed the garlic bread crumbs from his fingers as one of his dispatchers, Georgia Marks, tilted her head around the door frame of his office door.

"Hey, Chief." Georgia stood on one foot poised to run back to her dispatch cubicle if the radio went off.

"Yeah?"

"Wink said to tell you that it's all good." Georgia paused to see if Conrad showed recognition in his face and nodded.

"Okay, Georgie. Thanks." Looking up, he saw Georgia had run off without a sound from her thick rubber-soled shoes.

Conrad assumed Wink was conveying that the stop sign was replaced. He wasn't surprised. Cora always took care of business.

Saucy was a character, but he had a pure heart. He wasn't trying to be a pest and most of his wishes were simple things. His persistence made it futile to ignore the requests and the fact he was usually right about what needed to be done caused additional angst. He actually meant to help them do their jobs, but sometimes Conrad felt like groaning when he saw him sitting in the office waiting on him. Regretting his reaction, he was certain Cora felt the same. They had dealt with Saucy for many years.

When his phone rang, he expected it might be Wink relaying the message again. Wink never trusted Georgia to do anything.

"Chief Harris here."

"Well, hello Connie. How the heck are you?" The words were laced with insincerity and the sound of Bobby Bell's voice made the satisfied result of Conrad's dinner turn unsettled.

"Very well, Sheriff. What can I do for you this holiday evening?" Conrad tried to put a smile to his words. He was not going to let Bobby's evil spirit invade him. Things had been going well so far, and it had been dark for several hours.

"Got a little issue here and just wanted to get the word around— Not that it would necessarily involve you, but the county has had a theft tonight and they're running."

"You think they're running this way? Do you have a description I can put out to patrol?"

"No, we've got no description. Someone made off with the county fireworks display. We just know it's gone."

Conrad was alarmed yet had to stifle a guffaw at the same time. Someone had stolen Bobby's party toys and a part of him was delighted. The fact that someone might bring all that fire power into his town however, made him sit a bit uncomfortable.

"I'll get the word out to patrol." The word was they had nothing, but Conrad swallowed his cutting remarks. If the tables were turned, Bobby Bell wouldn't be as professional but he'd take the high road. Whoever stole the truck full of rockets and flares couldn't use them without being found very quickly.

Conrad called Wink on his cell phone and shared the sheriff's news. He didn't want it going out on the radio but he wanted patrol to be aware. Wink would get the word around where it needed to go. Saucy wasn't the only one in town with a scanner and he didn't want to be the news source reporting Bobby Bell's failure. He'd let the newspapers take that credit.

He got up to stretch his legs and clean his coffee cup when his phone rang again. Dispatch had been taxed all evening with calls about illegal fireworks. It happened every year. He only hoped someone wasn't reaching out to him about that.

"Chief Harris," he barked into the phone hoping to convey he was too busy for petty matters.

"Chief, I got a little added info that I wanted to pass on." Conrad froze at the sound of the sheriff's voice again. He really didn't want to get involved in his problem. They had never worked well together and whatever came of this would somehow become his fault.

"What do you have?"

"Well, we're hearing it may have been a white pickup that hooked up the flatbed and drove off. A lady living out on Eagle Bay said she thought she saw a white pickup go by pulling a bed and maybe back again."

There were only four occupied homes out on that road and no through traffic. If they pulled back out, they had to go to Paxton or Spicetown and a thief wouldn't go back to the scene of the crime.

"So, you're thinking they might be coming into Spicetown? I'll have everyone keep an eye out and call if we see anything."

"Thanks, Connie. I appreciate it." Bobby almost sounded sincere. Maybe he was realizing this theft would make a fool of him when he had to cancel the display. He only had an hour until show time.

"Oh—ah, Connie. No radio traffic on this, okay?"

"Of course not," Conrad assured him. It was a shame Bobby couldn't be this humble all the time. He might be tolerable to work with.

Conrad disconnected and called Wink again to relay the new details to him for patrol. The white pickup was rippling through his mind and he thought he might just drive around himself for a while. Putting his glasses back in his shirt pocket and hitching up his pants, he grabbed his jacket and headed out.

Eagle Bay was just outside of Spicetown city limits offering lake access to the few remaining houses. Conrad had spent hours down there when he had first moved to town. Bing, Cora Mae's late husband, had shown him the prime fishing holes. He was acquainted with the locals and was pretty sure he could guess who reported seeing the truck drive by.

Taking the rounded corner off the main highway to follow Eagle Bay Road, he spotted a county patrol car parked exactly where he expected— at Hazel Linton's house. That was where the deputy needed to be and Conrad coasted quietly by, hoping to pass unnoticed.

At the end of Eagle Bay Road there was a circle turnaround in sandy soil that offered an easy way to return to the highway, but those familiar with the area knew there was an unofficial boat launch nearby. Fishermen used it all the time to get their small boats in the water and time had worn the slope down to a smooth angle.

Conrad had fond memories of his time spent here and looked to see if the entry was still clear. He hoped to make time this spring to fish again. He hadn't gone since Bing had passed away and he missed the easy relaxation those memories brought to his mind.

The overgrowth of weeds and bushes near the path off the circle showed tire treads pressed into the ground. Conrad turned his car to push through to the clearing. Rolling down the window, he aimed the spotlight at the lake. The front edge of a black flatbed trailer was sticking up out of the water. The lake was too unsettled for his light to penetrate so he couldn't be sure, but he would bet the trailer full of fireworks had been released down the ramp and slipped into the water.

There were a few different ways he could handle this, so he analyzed his options. This wasn't his jurisdiction, and he didn't want to explain why he was here. Even more, he didn't want to call Bobby.

Ultimately, he chose the one option that kept him out of the limelight and drove to Hazel's house to wait patiently. When the young patrolman came out, he told him that he might want to check the boat launch area and left giving the deputy just enough information to stumble upon it himself. Heading back to Spicetown, he had one more place to check.

Chapter Three

Conrad's cruiser floated down Paprika Parkway in silence. He had always loved patrol on the midnight shift when all the good people were tucked in at home and any motion detected was suspect. He missed the stealth-like movements a cruiser made down a dark deserted street. All the bad would scurry away in hiding only to be discovered when he circled back for a second look. Although working nights could bring rushes of adrenaline when things went awry, it was otherwise a calming time for him. He loved both the highs and the lows.

He turned to drift down Dill Seed Drive and saw the new street sign that Cora Mae had quickly resolved. She was a fixer of things. He had worried a little about working for her when she became the mayor. He hadn't thought she would last, but he hadn't really known Cora Mae Bingham back then.

Her husband, George Bingham, had hired Conrad, and they had worked well together. Seeing that old fishing hole off Eagle Bay had brought back good memories of Old Bing. He was well liked and had held the position of Mayor for decades before Conrad came to town. He had introduced Conrad to almost every citizen in town, followed by a funny story, a touching anecdote or an explanation of their family tree. Bing had supported Conrad in the decisions he made regarding the police force and became a friend who he greatly respected. He missed his friend.

After Bing's death, Cora Mae retired from teaching and took Bing's job as mayor, easily winning re-election at the end of the term. In hindsight, she might even be a better mayor than her late spouse and she was becoming just as good a friend.

Conrad's headlights lit the driveway to Saucy's house when Dill Seed Drive met Sage Street. The house was dark, but Saucy's white truck was sitting in the driveway in front of the garage. Conrad killed his lights as he coasted into the drive behind it. Sliding out of the vehicle without shutting the door completely, he touched his hand to the back runner of the pickup and found it wet. Creeping around to the hood, he put his hand out and felt heat from the engine. The truck had been out tonight.

Conrad flinched as flood lights came on all around the house and Saucy flew out the side door.

"Oh, Chief! I'm so glad you got here. I've been hearing all kinds of things out here tonight and I just called Georgie. She told me to turn my lights on and someone would come by and check. You must have been really close. I don't know why I didn't have my lights on anyway. I know better. I just wasn't thinking. It's such a crazy night and these neighborhood kids are making me a nervous wreck. Did you see anyone? All this popping and snapping, I just can't take it."

"Take a deep breath, Saucy. It's New Year's Eve, and it's almost midnight. The noises are probably going to get worse here in a bit, but it will pass. It's too cold for you to be out here without a coat."

"I can't sleep until everything calms down. I wish people wouldn't set off these fireworks. Aren't they illegal? Can't you stop them?"

"We try. We try to answer every call."

"Why do people like those things? They're horrible. Nothing good ever comes from them and they scare my little dog to death. I just hate them." Saucy held up a finger while he slipped in the door and grabbed a jacket. "So, you didn't see anything when you drove up? I know I heard something out here."

"No, but I see you got your stop sign fixed. When did they do that?"

"Oh, yes. The mayor had it put up before I even got home tonight. I was so relieved."

"You went out tonight?"

"Well, yes. Just for dinner, of course. It's Tuesday and I always go to Ole' Thyme on Tuesdays. And the sign was already up when I got home. Can you believe it? She works so fast."

"Yes, I believe it," Conrad shifted his feet against the gravel of the drive. "What time did you get home?"

"Oh, I don't know, maybe 7:00 or so. It was still quiet outside at least then but it's been unsettling since about 9:00. I didn't want to call and bother you. I heard Wink, and I knew he was all the way out at Nutmeg Lane. I didn't realize you were out patrolling tonight, too. I guess you had to with all the calls and the"

"Saucy, do you always leave your truck out? It's not supposed to snow tonight, but you never know. You wouldn't want it to get covered up." Conrad had always seen Saucy's truck inside the garage in the past.

"I don't know why I didn't put it up tonight. I'm just so rattled with all this."

Conrad tapped the flat of his hand against the hood of the truck twice. "I've got to get going. It's just about to hit midnight. You get inside and get warm." Saucy was still nodding as Conrad backed out of the drive.

§

Conrad went into the office on New Year's Day. There had been a few pity invites for family dinners from patrolmen, but he didn't fit into those situations. For him there was only work and food. From the size of his belly he thought he needed to go to work.

Checking in with his skeletal holiday staff, he heard all the tales from their New Year's Eve calls. One boy had been burned by improper handling of illegal fireworks, but there were no fatalities reported so he was happy to put the holiday behind him. The populace would never learn.

He'd been awake half the night thinking about his talk with Saucy but he wasn't ready to share that with anyone yet, not even Wink. Conrad was surprised by the number of people out walking around town when he drove up, but it was a mild winter day with sunshine sneaking out through the clouds. Quite cheerful for a winter day and a nice change from the solid cloud cover they were used to in winter. Some small businesses were having sales beginning today, and it had drawn a good crowd.

Conrad strolled down Paprika Parkway passing City Hall and saw Cora's car parked in the back. She was supposed to be off from work today, too. He might try talking to her about Saucy but he had to think on it a bit. Cora wasn't law enforcement, and she had a different take on things than Wink. Wink would want to call the sheriff and that was the last thing Conrad wanted to think about.

He turned on Fennel Street and caught the rush of cold wind whipping down the sidewalk in front of the Fennel Street Bakery. When a patron walked out, the scent of cinnamon followed behind them. He would just get coffee and think on things a bit more. Pulling the door handle back, the warm yeast aroma of the bakery floated around him and like comfortable arms, it pulled him into the store.

Several of the small counter high tables that surrounded the walls were occupied, and he greeted those he knew but right in the center at a large round table sat Cora Mae Bingham with her glasses on her nose and her necklace chain dangling down while she furiously wrote in her leather binder. She was the queen of note taking and was constantly recording and organizing thoughts. She didn't even look up when he approached.

"Can I warm up that coffee for you, ma'am," Conrad said smiling. She was in another world of city planning and he saw he flustered her by interrupting.

Glancing up over the top of her glasses, a broad smile emerged. "Connie! I thought you might wander in here. Get yourself something and join me."

"I don't want to interrupt the re-invention of Spicetown." She was always planning a makeover of every nuance of the town and had big dreams. It had been the topic of many conversations. Perhaps he'd unconsciously expected her to be here, too.

"Nonsense. I'll just write you right into my plans."

The warm smile was welcoming, and he went to the counter to order his coffee and maybe a muffin to go with it. Cora ran her fingers through her ginger-colored hair and quickly concluded her last note to herself. The list was endless and she would never run out of things to do.

"So, what committee are you signing me up for?" Conrad pulled out the chair next to Cora. "I'm up for anything. It's a new year."

"Well, I have a list of possibilities," she said anticipating the teasing he would give her about her lists.

"As long as I don't have to dress up in any silly costume, I'm game."

Cora read her lists to him of all the many things she wanted to do and he listened intently. A question was coming.

"So, if you could only do two of these things, which two would you pick?"

"You will accomplish more than two things this year," Conrad said.

"Unless I get hit by a truck, I hope so, but this question is to help me prioritize the list. I never get everything done so I have to work on the most important things first."

"What would you do if you got everything done?" Conrad pulled his glasses out of his shirt pocket and took the list from her hand to review. It was too long for him to remember everything she read to him. "I don't see anything about raises for all the police department employees on here."

He smiled as he looked over the top of his glasses at her.

"I consider that a fringe benefit and it's on my list of things to do with found money."

Conrad nodded, accepting that this was probably true. She would do something for his people if and when she could. She valued all of them.

"I think I'd put the renovation of the popcorn factory first because it would be revenue generating and then replace the sewer pipe before disaster hits."

"A practical choice." Cora took back her list and lifted her glasses from her neck chain. As the waitress warmed her coffee, she shuffled some papers back into her leather folder. "So, how did New Year's Eve go? Was it quiet?"

"I wouldn't call any New Year's Eve quiet, but nothing burned down and we got through it."

"That's good news. Pretty sneaky of you to send Saucy to me at the end of the day." Cora squinted her eyes and wrinkled her nose in mock frustration.

"You're just sore I beat you to it." Conrad winked, which made Cora smile and nod in agreement. "You got it done for him though. I saw it later that night. Where did Saucy go when he left your office?"

"I don't know. I went home, and he didn't say he was going anywhere. Why? Wasn't he home last night?"

"Later, before midnight he was there, but I think he was out earlier. Just wondered if he mentioned anything."

"Nope, not a thing to me. I heard the county had to cancel their fireworks display. The radio mentioned it this morning, but I didn't catch what happened. Did you hear anything about it?"

"Yeah, I heard it was called off," Conrad looked around the room for someone to greet or acknowledge. He wasn't going to spread tales about Bobby's embarrassing night. Cora would eventually find out on her own. "Saucy was sure jumpy last night," Conrad said smiling. "Holidays always make him nervous."

"He's gotten worse as he's gotten older. The neighborhood boys taunting him doesn't help." Conrad stared across the room when the details of the prior evening filled his mind again.

"I think he has a lot of fears and feels vulnerable being alone. When he was married, he would have run outside and scared those kids off, but now he's afraid they will retaliate."

"Did his wife die?"

"No, she just ran off. It's been probably twenty years ago or more now. I guess they divorced, and she moved away. I didn't know him well back then, and he never talks about it. Seems like she had a child, a girl, but it wasn't Saucy's."

Conrad glanced at his vibrating phone and saw Wink's name. Using the call to excuse himself, he paid at the counter and headed back to the office, wishing Cora a good day.

Listening to the voice mail as he walked back, Wink was just calling to invite him over again. Wink wasn't working today, and he didn't want Conrad to spend all day at the office. Pizza and football didn't sound bad, but he wasn't ready to talk about last night yet, so he thought it best to just keep to himself today. He did want to know whether or not the submerged trailer had held the fireworks. Dispatch should know that much, so he headed back to the office.

Saucy was such a stickler for following laws and rules. Could Saucy have stolen the fireworks? You had to be pretty daring to do something like that and that just didn't describe Saucy. He had been somewhere though and hadn't been home long. He had lied about it when Conrad asked, so he was hiding something. He hated fireworks so maybe he just went to the display to complain about them and saw a chance to ruin them. If he was passionate enough about it, he might have done it.

As he walked by Ivy's Oils & Organics, he saw Saucy through the window at the side counter talking to Denise Ivy. It seemed an odd place for him since it sold mainly essential oils and soaps, but there was no one else in the store that he could see. Denise lived near Saucy and the neighborhood kids harassed her, too. They called her a witch and said she sold magic potions. She had reported some vandalism around her house. Maybe they were talking about that. Conrad needed to tell Wink to increase patrols in their area for a while.

Walking back to the office, Conrad looked for a newspaper but the sidewalk rack was empty. Maybe there wasn't a paper printed today because it was a holiday. He wasn't sure but walked in the side door of the police department and headed for dispatch.

"Hey Georgie. Did we get a paper today? Do they even print one today?"

Before she could answer, she got a radio call and Conrad had to wait. He looked around the office and shuffled papers thinking today's paper might be covered up under there somewhere.

"What's up, Chief?" Georgia said when she finished her call.

"Did you ever hear anything more about the county fireworks situation last night? Did they find them? Or did they send any follow-up information out?"

"Nope. I haven't heard a thing."

"Okay, thanks," Conrad said as he headed back down the hall to his office and removed his coat. Surely if they had found the fireworks, they would have released that in the news, even if they didn't have a suspect. Maybe he'd been wrong and that trailer hitch in the lake wasn't from the flatbed of fireworks. The next time he got out, he was going to drive out there and see if it was still there.

He took off his coat and sat down at his desk to check online for news.

"Hey, Chief," Wink said as he rounded the corner of Conrad's office door with his dog, Hank. "I thought I'd find you here."

Conrad regretted not calling him back. Hank pulled at the leash to try to reach Conrad. When he nodded, Wink dropped the leash and let him lunge at the Chief for a vigorous scratch behind the ears. If Wink wasn't working, he had Hank with him and Hank had always loved Conrad.

"Hey. What brings you up here?" Conrad knew the answer, of course. Wink didn't know what to do when he wasn't working either.

"Just coming to town for a few things. Did you get my message? Want to knock off this afternoon and watch the game?"

"I just got your message. I was out getting breakfast. I think I'm going to stick around here most of the day. I don't really care for either team so I'm going to skip it this year I think."

Wink nodded and shuffled his feet with his hands in his coat pockets.

"Do they print a paper on New Year's Day?" Conrad looked up and saw Wink perplexed. "I looked for one on Fennel Street and couldn't find one. There's not one in dispatch either. Maybe they don't print one today."

"Maybe not," Wink said. "Did you hear back from Sheriff Bell on that fireworks thing last night?"

"No, didn't hear anything more." Conrad didn't want to go there with Wink. He could always wiggle himself into Conrad's thoughts and he wasn't ready to share his concerns yet. "I went home about 1:00am. Anything happen much after that?"

"No, it quieted down pretty quick. Lots of folks went to the county display, and they went home peacefully once they came back. I did see something odd before midnight though that I wanted to run by you."

"Sure thing. Have a seat," Conrad said as he removed his glasses and stretched back in his chair, glancing at his coffee maker with longing.

"When you called me and told me what the Sheriff said, I got to thinking. I saw a white truck in the alley earlier that night, but when I went back, it wasn't there anymore. I thought it odd when I saw it, but there's nothing illegal about parking. It was that alley off Clove Street, but I can't remember what time. It was dark, but it was before you called me. I'm pretty sure it was a Ford truck. Did the Sheriff say what make the truck was?"

"No, I don't even know the source. It may not have been a solid lead." Could it have been Saucy? The alley off Clove Street ran behind the stores on Fennel Street and Tarragon Street. All of those stores closed at 5:00. Nothing would have been open after Wink's shift began, but it might be a store owner or delivery coming in after closing.

"I went by Saucy's right before midnight. He thought someone was lurking around his property. You know Denise Ivy has had some problems over there on Sage Street, too. I think we need to increase patrols around there for a bit," Conrad said as Wink nodded. It may just be kids but a car might tone them down.

"Sure thing, boss. I'll let the guys know," Wink backed out the door and headed down the hall with Hank.

Saucy's truck was a Ford, but he had no reason to be at a business after hours. He wondered if Saucy had decided to start his own patrolling of the town and maybe that's why it was warm when he stopped by last night. No reason to lie about that though. It probably had nothing to do with fireworks. Saucy wouldn't steal anything. That just wasn't in him.

§

Cora went back to City Hall and let herself in the back door. There were no employees in today because of the holiday and she thought she'd just take advantage of the silence and type up her notes. Anything she could do today would make tomorrow easier.

The hall had a different feeling when she was there alone. The big lobby echoed her footsteps when she walked across the highly polished wood floor and the high wooden counter looked bleak with no computer monitors glowing. She saw a large vase with red roses sitting on the end of the counter that she hadn't noticed yesterday. There was a card with Amanda's name on it clipped to a plastic spike. They were still fresh and open so they must have come late yesterday and she had forgotten to take them home.

The floor creaked as she walked around the counter and headed to her office. The sun was bright today, so she opened the large heavy venetian blinds and let the light fill her office. Turning on her computer, she dug out the lists from her large satchel. She had made some decisions she needed to commit to writing for the coming year. One of the things she wanted to add back to the budget was a firework display for the fourth of July and she hoped to unveil her statue of John Spicer at the same time. She was going to contact the sheriff tomorrow and ask about the New Year's Eve display. Conrad obviously didn't want to talk about it, but she'd rather the county handle that next year so she didn't have to budget it. The theft may lead the county to decide they didn't want to hold the event again. Cora would use that as an excuse to find out what happened. She wasn't at all ashamed of being more than a little curious.

Sheri Richey

Chapter Four

Ivy's Oils & Organics was a small shop on Fennel Street just two doors down from the Fennel Street Bakery. Denise Ivy had opened it last summer primarily to market essential oils, which she strongly believed could cure any ailment. She soon found she needed an additional draw and added organic lotions and soaps to her offerings. Her attempt to make the store a success had cost her all of her savings.

As the bell over the door chimed, Denise slapped on her happy greeter face to try it one more time. "Welcome to Ivy's Oils. Is there anything particular I can help you find today?"

Two ladies entered cautiously and looked around. Denise's heart sank because they were older ladies she didn't think would be open minded enough to try her natural remedies, but the scented soaps might work on them.

"Oh, no. We're just looking around some. It smells lovely in here." The taller lady smiled sweetly. Denise thanked them and they walk over to the soaps and lotions as she expected.

Her mother had warned her not to move back to Spicetown and said opening this store was a mistake. Her friends and family didn't feel she could be an effective sales person.

Denise didn't know the best way to busy herself when customers were browsing. Should she try to talk to steer them toward products they needed or should she leave them alone? Maybe she needed to be bolder.

"Have you ladies ever used essential oils? They are really helpful as natural remedies."

The two ladies looked at each other in puzzlement. "Why, no. I wouldn't know what to do with them," the taller lady said looking quizzically at her companion.

"Well," Denise sighed and took the plunge. "They can treat bug bites, help with cold symptoms, moisturize your skin, scent your home safely and improve brain focus and clarity. Do you need help with any of those things?"

"My goodness," the shorter lady exclaimed. The bright red scarf tied around her neck brought out her rosy cheeks. "I thought you just used them to make these soaps."

"They can be used to scent products. I have a recipe over here that shows how you can make your own gel air fresheners for your home. They smell divine and there are no toxic chemicals in them for you to breathe in, like when you buy air fresheners at a store. It just takes unflavored gelatin and salt." Denise handed them a free copy of the recipe. "You can add food coloring for effect, but the oils are suspended in the gelatin and stay smelling wonderful for months."

"Now, Libby," the taller lady said. "You love your scented candles. You could make something like this. It looks simple."

The smaller lady considered it. "But what scent do I use?"

"Oh, you can pick your favorite or you can combine them," Denise said excitedly. "I love the pumpkin pie scent in the fall and a flower garden in the spring. What scent of candles do you usually choose?"

"Oh, I got all kinds. Maybe some springtime might be a good thing. I'm about ready for the winter to lift."

Denise pulled the lavender, geranium and grapefruit from the display and opened each sample display bottle for her to smell. Then she offered her a gel candle in a mason jar to smell the three together. "This is what it makes," she said proudly.

"Hmm, I don't know if I'd ever get around to doing all that," the smaller lady said, shaking her head.

Denise's hopes deflated, but she fought back. "You don't have to mix anything. If you find a fragrance you like, you can just use a single oil." Denise reached for the clove, but the lady curled up her lip, so she picked up the lavender again. "Lavender is one of the scents that improves concentration and focus. It's also very calming. You can make scented gel from this and also put a couple of drops on your wrist or neck to relax your body and sharpen your mind."

"I'll give it a try, young lady," the smaller lady said with a wink and a smile. Denise felt relief flood her tense shoulders. Maybe she could do this after all.

The taller lady bought a body lotion, and she sold the scent to her friend putting a few informational handouts in the bags along with their products. She felt strongly education was all that was necessary to convince people they needed these oils. They had changed her life, and she wanted everyone to benefit as she had.

After seeing the ladies off, Denise wondered how she could find a voice in the community to tell people about these great products. There had to be somewhere she could find a platform to teach. Now that she'd found a way to cut some costs with her products, she might succeed if business would improve.

As Denise tidied the shelf, she congratulated herself again for taking the risk to repackage the lower quality oils to sell for crafts. The increased margin made a big difference in her bottom line.

This little lady with the red scarf might never even use her oil or if she did, it would just be to make an air freshener, so she sold her the diluted low-quality oil. This might be the only way she could keep the store open. Denise told herself she didn't feel guilty at all.

§

Bryan Stotlar threw another log on his fire and went in the kitchen to warm up his coffee. With the holidays over and no snow in the forecast, he didn't have anything urgent to tend to. He sat down and watched the cat curled near the fireplace; he wished he had been born a cat. Life was so easy for cats. No complicated social interactions, no politics to work around or feelings to hurt. They ate when it was available and slept it off. He would love a simple life like that.

Turning his family land into a tree farm had seemed a great idea when he was twenty. Now the reality of how limiting it was weighed on his heart. He had struggled with several options for the future and decided the only practical thing was to expand the concept into a full nursery of plants and increase his knowledge of landscaping.

To add to his despondency, his date last night with Amanda Morgan hadn't left him feeling confident. Everything seemed to go so smoothly until they got in his truck and he couldn't think of anything to say. She had a bubbly personality and tried to keep the conversation engaging, but Bryan couldn't keep up his end of the deal. He was nervous about driving, about parking, about whether she was warm enough, about whether she wanted the radio on and his inner voice was making fun of all his petty concerns. By the time they were seated at The Barberry Tower for dinner, his confidence was gone.

Although he had experienced this deflating loss of personality before in other encounters, it had never mattered so much. Amanda was really important to him. She was the first woman he had ever worked so hard to connect with and make an impression.

As their food arrived at the table, Bryan remembered his mother's words to him when he was in high school. *Ask her about herself and talk about her interests. Girls want to know you want to know them.*

Fueled with positive nostalgia, Bryan asked her about college, about her wishes for her future, about her job and her favorite things. Once again, his mother had saved him. Funny how he never listened to her when she was alive.

Amanda's tales had been foreign to him. She had lived a very different life. He hadn't gone to college and hadn't participated in parties or events as Amanda had. Living on a farm didn't provide him with fascinating stories to tell. He enjoyed hearing about her life, but he couldn't relate to it. Bryan had nothing to add, so he nodded often and withdrew further.

The time passed, and he hadn't even remembered to enjoy it. He had let his anxiety consume him and instead of relishing those precious moments of sharing a meal with Amanda Morgan, he had conceded defeat before they even left the restaurant.

Arriving at the county fairgrounds had relieved some pressure from him because Amanda was friends with a number of people in the gathering crowd. Acquaintances from school and from City Hall were seeking her out. She never seemed to hesitate to engage with people, even those she had never met before. Floating around the crowd to greet others, she always returned to him. She tried to be polite, but each time they were quickly interrupted by another reunion.

Learning that the fireworks display was being canceled was a relief. His vision of snuggling with Amanda in the cold and getting a New Year's kiss were pure fantasy, so ending the evening earlier was saving his dignity. He was horribly disappointed, but not in the event cancellation. He was disappointed in himself.

Cats never had these problems.

Sheri Richey

Chapter Five

"Good morning, Jimmy," Cora called out as she stomped her feet on the doormat inside the back door of City Hall. Jimmy Kole's office was nearest the employee's entrance in the back of City Hall because all the city street department workers came in and out frequently. They could be a little messy at times.

"Morning, Mayor," Jimmy called back as she hung up her coat. "Happy New Year!"

"You sound ready to get started," Cora said looking in his doorway with a smile. She enjoyed his eagerness and willingness to try new things. She needed new vigor around her because the City Council was full of old stuffy citizens that criticized every proposal she brought and feared every whiff of change. Jimmy loved a new challenge and always embraced change. He would make an excellent council member someday.

"I am. I'm sure you have lots of new ideas to go with the new year."

"I have a few I'm considering. We'll have a meeting soon and see what we can do." Cora had a twinkle in her eye and felt energized just with the brief conversation. Her staff was just the opposite of the City Council. They were excited by a challenge just as she was. She would enjoy that as long as she could.

"Good morning, Mayor," the girls at the counter said as she entered the lobby. Everyone was cheerful and sharing stories about their New Year's Eve. They immediately asked her if she'd heard about the fireworks cancellation, looking for details about what happened. She was curious about that, too. She promised to share if she found out details and the girls returned to their workstations still chattering like little birds.

"Good morning," Amanda said as Cora walked through her office to get to her own. "I hope you had a nice holiday."

"Yes, it was a nice break. And how was your New Year's Eve?"

"Well, the fireworks were canceled, but I had a nice time. Do you know what happened?"

"No, I just heard they were canceled. So, what did you do instead?" Amanda hadn't directly shared the information that she had a date with Bryan Stotlar, but she must know Cora had heard from the other employees. "Did you and Bryan have a nice evening?"

"Yes, it was just cut short. We went to dinner and I really don't like fireworks much anyway, but it kind of messed up the date."

"Well, that can be fixed with the next one," Cora said smiling to see if Amanda reacted favorably.

"I don't know if there will be one. It was kind of awkward."

"Come on in," Cora motioned to her to go in her office with her so they could sit down. Amanda looked like she wanted to talk and it really wasn't something she could do with her own mother, so Cora didn't mind standing in. Amanda's mother, Louise Morgan, ran a hair salon in town and anything shared with her mother went viral around town.

"So, what was awkward? Did you two not get along?"

"Oh, no. It wasn't that. I was just nervous, and I talked constantly. He couldn't get a word in and I talked about myself all night. Looking back, I'm just so embarrassed. I don't know what got into me. When he found out the fireworks were canceled, he just took me home. He didn't say anything about seeing me again." Amanda put her head down in her hands. "I don't think I can even face him."

"I don't know Bryan well, but he seems relatively shy and quiet. It's hard to read other people's mind, but it's even harder to do that with people who don't talk much. I'm sure it wasn't as bad as you think."

"Trust me. It was." Amanda looked up smiling and shaking her head as the humiliation lingered.

"He was probably nervous, too. You turned him down the first time, so he might have been on edge about that. I bet he was relieved you were talking, so he didn't have to think of something to say."

"Maybe," Amanda said thoughtfully. "He did ask a lot of questions like he really wanted to know about me. We'll see."

"Why did you turn him down the first time?" Amanda seemed to care about the impression she made, so this wasn't a simple date, as she'd first thought.

"I really didn't. I mean I didn't mean to," Amanda said holding her hands up in disbelief. "I thought he was joking and again, I got nervous and blabbered something that made him think I was saying no. I just made a mess of things then too."

"He tried twice then. I bet he tries again, too," Cora said with a sparkle in her eyes. Amanda was especially cute when she was nervous and blabbering on, and the possibility of young love warmed Cora's heart. She remembered that nervous twittering it gave her when Bing came near. Bing always made her giggle like an idiot and she would regret it later but repeat it the next time he paid any attention to her. She missed Bing so deeply that it hurt.

"Oh, well," Amanda sighed and stood up. "What's on our agenda this year?"

"Well, I've been working on that but I'm not ready to set the agenda for the Council meeting yet. I will be soon, but I need to do a bit of research yet."

"I'll let you get to it, then. Let me know if you need anything." Amanda turned to go back to her desk.

"If you see Chief Harris come in, let me know."

"Okay," Amanda said as she shut Cora's door.

Cora thought again about Bryan Stotlar. She knew she had him as a student years ago, but she just couldn't remember a thing about him. She always remembered her students, either for positive or negative reasons, but something about each of them. It was very unusual for a fifth-grade boy to sit in class for a full school year and not make a good or bad memory for her.

Of course, she had known his parents. Bing had always enjoyed visiting their farm even though they didn't live within Spicetown city limits. He had always told Cora about his visits even though she rarely went with him. He made all the townspeople her personal friends too, just in the retelling of all his encounters.

Some of that had changed with Bing's passing though. The death of a spouse was not like any other loss. It had changed the rhythm in her daily life. Her comfortable routine was gone. The way she woke up in the morning, the meals she ate, the events she attended and her circle of friends had all changed. She had been handed a life she did not want, and she had to change to fit into it. She had taken his job in the hopes that it would keep some of him with her but being mayor of Spicetown had taken on a whole new meaning with Cora behind it.

With Bing gone, she always turned to Connie. Conrad Harris had been her husband's choice for Chief of Police and he had shared much of Conrad's professional past with Cora so she had an unfair advantage. She knew him before they ever met. Connie was someone she could always share thoughts with in complete trust. She kept his thoughts, and he kept hers. Consequently, they knew each other well, although most people didn't realize that.

Chapter Six

Conrad showed up late to work because he had patrolled late into the night. That niggling feeling was still there, and he had wanted to see what was happening around town on his own. It wasn't that he didn't trust Wink to handle things, but there were still things that Wink didn't know.

He had driven out to Eagle Bay Road and looked at the hidden boat launch. Under the beam of his flashlight, he saw fresh tire ruts. The flatbed was gone. He was sure he had seen it, so the county must have pulled it out and taken it to Paxton. He would never know if there was anything on it now. Maybe they found the fireworks and had decided to keep it quiet. If so, it would come out eventually. If it wasn't there why take the flatbed away at all?

Pride was poison to law enforcement. You had to accept what happened and face it. Sure, it would have been uncomfortable to report to the community that county products were stolen right out from under the sheriff's nose when he was on duty at the site. Conrad wouldn't have hidden it though. He knew those things always came out, and it was harder to face if you looked like you were trying to deceive. Bobby Bell had more pride than good sense.

Conrad had driven by Saucy's house a dozen times throughout the night and never saw anything. Saucy appeared to be home, his truck was parked in the driveway again rather than the garage, but he saw no movement. He drove up and down Fennel Street and never saw a white truck in any of the alleys. He accomplished nothing, and the niggling was not calmed. Maybe it was time to talk to someone about it.

Conrad took off his coat and heard chatter down at dispatch but he didn't feel like joining in. He went straight to his coffee maker, and the ritual began. Once the cinnamon and French vanilla creamer were mixed to perfection, he breathed deeply. He wasn't sure which was better, the smell or the taste. He was grateful he had the benefit of both.

Once his computer was up, he looked for news on the county fireworks and found nothing. The newspapers were reporting the unfortunate cancellation but must not have gotten any information before they went to press. He did see a comment on one of the articles where citizens were sharing the rumor that the fireworks were stolen. There had been a lot of local thefts in the

Paxton area recently and that further fueled the rumor. With public speculation, the press would demand more. A news release was probably imminent.

Wink's shift didn't start until evening so Conrad would update him when he came in. He was going to move on after that. Maybe his barometer was off this time. Everything had seemed peaceful last night and there were other things to worry about in Spicetown.

Conrad checked on the police reports from last night and took a stroll around downtown. Spicetown was small. Small enough that he felt like he knew everyone, yet just big enough that a stranger passed by and made him wonder. There were some folks from Paxton or other neighboring towns that visited regularly and even some tourists once in a while, so the downtown did show new faces.

Cora had told him that some people thought they made spices here and were coming because they felt the quality was superior. It was one of her pet peeves. She felt it was false advertising, and it had put her at odds with the Chamber of Commerce president when she objected to some of their town marketing that implied spices originated there.

Cora loved to tell the story about how Spicetown was named for a man named John Spicer, who had worked on the railroad. After several years of traveling through the area, he picked this spot to call his home. He was an

- 49 -

entrepreneur and used inventive ways to attract others traveling the railroad to join him, eventually growing enough that they made the railroad stop there. The depot was labeled Spicer's, which eventually grew into Spicetown.

The townspeople had enjoyed naming the streets to coincide with spices which created a trend for the businesses to join in. Somehow over the years, Spicetown made the map and the eclectic spicy choices drew some curious visitors.

Cora had always wanted to erect a statue of John Spicer and tell his story, but the Council had always stopped her. They claimed they didn't want to spend the money, but Cora told him that they wanted the truth kept quiet. She felt that Miriam Landry, the Chamber of Commerce president, had them on her shady side.

Either way, the folks of Spicetown did know the truth because the mayor told them every chance she got. Conrad had to chuckle just thinking about it. Cora Mae could sure get riled up once in a while.

Strolling down Fennel Street, he looked in the storefronts and saw the bustle of yesterday had died. The Fennel Street Bakery had a couple of coffee drinkers and Ivy's Oils & Organics was empty. The Caraway Cafe did have several tables filled, and he was ready for lunch. Patting his belly, he thought he might need to eat a little lighter today. He had snacked all evening on junk food and was still feeling it. He couldn't cook anything so he almost always dined out. He argued it was good exposure for the community to see him, but in reality, he could only heat soup. A man got tired of soup.

Waving to the hostess when he entered, he found a table near the front window to watch street traffic. Pulling his glasses from his shirt pocket, he perused the menu for something that he could categorize as light cuisine. Skipping over the salads completely, he decided on a grilled fish and waited for the server.

Several of the sidewalk strollers waved to him as they passed. Most were familiar people, but then he saw a man passing the Fennel Street Bakery that he didn't know. The man was short and slight in build but stomping out each step as though his destination would be reached quicker that way. His thin black hair covered his ears and out-shined his weather-beaten black leather jacket. Conrad couldn't decide if he was angry, late or just wanting to get out of the cold. He didn't glance in any of the storefronts so he had some destination in mind. Conrad was so engrossed in the deliberate little man that he didn't notice the waiter had approached.

"Chief?" Conrad jerked his head to the left and saw Georgia Marks' son in a serving apron with an order pad in hand. "Are you ready to order?"

"Hey, Jason," Conrad said and then looked out the window again to keep track of the little man. "Yes, I'll have the grilled fish platter with beans and slaw. Water to drink. Thanks."

"Do you know that guy?" Jason asked when he saw the man Conrad was watching.

"No, I've not seen him before."

"Well, he's been around for a couple of weeks now. I see him come and go every few days, but I don't know him. Maybe he's new in town." Jason slipped his pen back in his apron pocket. "I'll put your order in. Let me know if you need anything."

"Thanks, Jason," Conrad said nodding without looking at him. The man had crossed the street now and was walking up to Denise Ivy's store. There was no hesitation in his step so that was his intended destination. He could see in one window of Ivy's Oils & Organics from his seat but could only tell that Denise didn't come out from behind the counter to greet her visitor. Conrad got up and switched to the other side of his window table so he could comfortably keep an eye on her door.

Conrad's meal arrived, and the man was still in Ivy's. If he remained once he finished, he was going over there to check it out. As he trained his eyes on Ivy's store entrance, Cora Mae Bingham crossed his line of vision and waved through the window at him. He returned the greeting and was unsurprised when she rounded his table minutes later to seat herself across from him.

"Hi, Connie. Mind if I sit with you while you eat?"

"Of course not, Cora. Are you having lunch?"

"No, actually I was looking for you. Georgie told me you were down here."

Conrad didn't have to ask how she knew that. He had told Georgie he was going to eat but suspected his waiter had texted his mom to report he was serving the Chief. There were few secrets in a small town.

Conrad nodded his head as he chewed and Cora told Jason to bring her a cup of tea.

"So, who are we staking out?" Cora said in an exaggerated whisper.

Conrad smiled and waited to swallow to reply. "Just keeping an eye on Denise's place over there. Saw a strange little guy go in there quite a while ago and he's not come out."

"Hmm," Cora said. "I should have brought my binoculars."

Conrad strangled a little on his last bite and reached for his water glass. Cora gave him an impish grin in apology.

"I wouldn't expect Denise to have a lot of business from strange little men. Her products are geared more towards women and the store is tiny. It wouldn't take long to see everything in there."

"My thoughts exactly," Conrad said.

"Here comes Saucy. He looks like he is going in Denise's too."

"Well, he peeked in the door and then backed away. He's headed past now. I wonder why," Conrad said trailing off into thought. "Why were you looking for me?"

"Oh, just being nosey," Cora said as she accepted her tea from Jason and added sugar. "I want to hear what happened with the fireworks. Rumors abound and I'd like to know the truth."

"I don't know much," Conrad said, looking first at Cora and back to the street. "You know Bobby and I don't chat much but he did call me Tuesday night and tell me someone lifted the merchandise. That's about all I know."

"Stolen, I'd heard some talk of that. Odd thing to steal, isn't it?"

"Sure is," Conrad said pushing his plate to the side. "Can't imagine what anyone wanted with them unless they just wanted to stop the display from happening or maybe were just pulling a prank."

"Pretty expensive prank," Cora huffed. "Those big shows don't come cheap. I was relieved the city didn't have to pay for any of it.

"I can imagine."

"I also wanted to ask you about Bryan Stotlar." Conrad looked directly at Cora then, surprised by the request.

"Bryan? What about him? He seems like a good guy. No trouble from him."

"Well, my assistant, Mandy, had a date with him on New Year's and I'm just curious. I don't really know anything about him at all and"

"And you know something about everyone," Conrad chuckled.

"Yes," Cora said demurely and stirred her tea. "I'm also being a bit of a fill-in mother hen. I love Amanda dearly and I don't want her"

"To get mixed up with the wrong kind of guy. Yeah, I know."

"Well, that's why I'm asking you. Because you do know," Cora said emphatically, trying to catch Conrad's eye as his focus was trained across the street.

"Nothing to tell, really. Bryan's a good kid. Never caused any trouble. He's trying to make a go of it in this town, just like Denise there," Conrad said pointing to Ivy's Oils & Organics. "That's tough on kids. He took his folks dying pretty hard, but he's starting to put it back together."

"He's a very quiet young man. Does he talk to you?"

"Yes, he's not talkative just to hear himself, but he's not hard to talk to. He took some trees over to a couple of houses this year that had folks who weren't able to get out. He set them up in the living room for them. You know the Winklemans out on Bay Leaf?" Cora nodded. "He took one to them and over to Ethel Baccus. I don't think he even charged them anything. He seems like a good guy. I don't think you have anything to worry about."

"Probably not," Cora said as she wrinkled her forehead. "I had him as a student and can't remember one thing about him. It's really bugging me, too. That never happens."

Conrad smiled and turned to look at Cora. He knew that puzzled look. There was no point in telling her she couldn't possibly remember every student because indeed she could. "He was probably just an average student, just quiet enough to stay off your radar."

"I guess," Cora said unconvincingly and pushed her chair back. "Why don't we go take a look around Ivy's Oils & Organics!"

Conrad nodded and Jason brought over his check.

Bundling up at the door to leave, Conrad turned to Cora. "Do you have a good reason to go in there?"

"Well," Cora glanced upward in thought. "I might need a birthday gift for a dear old friend?"

"Perfect," Conrad said yanking the door open for Cora to exit. "Let's go."

Chapter Seven

Bryan had deliveries on the way. He had used his profits from Christmas tree sales to invest in items to expand the tree farm into a nursery. Laying out his plans on the kitchen table, Bryan checked over his pending orders and expected deliveries. This was the first step toward his new goals and his father would be proud to know that.

His father had been the one that always had a vision, always could see years down the road. His mother lived for today. Unfortunately, Bryan was like his mother as a young man and his father had always been concerned about his future.

With both of them gone, he thanked his father every day for foreseeing he would need help in his future. He was going to pay him back by picking up the pieces and making something of this farm. Yearning for his father's advice wouldn't help; he already had it all in his memories. Time to put that advice to use.

When Bryan had been a young man, his father had asked him to plant an empty field on their property with Christmas trees. He told Bryan that he thought people in town would want to go back to the real thing in the future and the trees would be ready by then.

At the time, shiny tinsel and colored artificial trees were all the rage. People even purchased trees that already had lights on them. Everyone wanted the easy flashy fakes, not the traditional, but his father had told him that these trends never last. 'People veer off for a few years, but then they always come back to the place where their heart is.' They would want a real tree in their home with popcorn and homemade ornaments again.

Bryan had laughed at him, teased him, told him only the birds and the deer would thank him, but in the end, he had planted all the trees.

He knew now his father had been planning a future for him. His father had already been ill at that time and had to know he wouldn't be cutting and selling Christmas trees in ten years. Bryan cut hundreds every year and planted new ones. He tied them and set them up in front of the barn each November for sale. He worked hard to keep up with demand and the last few years had let the public on the lots to pick their own if they wanted. He was the only Christmas tree farm in town and everyone wanted one of his trees. His father had been right.

This trend would not last forever though. His father had always said interests were cyclical and he must change with the current cultural trends to stay successful.

Growing up, their farm had seen many changes. They had raised rabbits, goats, chickens and horses. They had grown vegetables, sold prepared canned preserves, offered a petting zoo for kids with tours for families and horseback trail rides. His father was always altering their life to stay afloat, yet the farm was still the farm.

With his parents' illness and passing, Bryan had been overwhelmed with the demands of the farm and had sold some livestock for immediate cash. Once he realized that he had to make his own way, he had tried to channel his father and focused on his future in a way he didn't know he could.

He began to grow herbs to sell to local restaurants and now that eating healthy had become popular, he sold some of his plants to specialty stores in town. He had begun drying some and packaging them to add to his spring shopping stand that he would open in March at the greenhouse.

The farm was a couple of miles from Spicetown and he had never imagined that people would drive out there to shop, but he had underestimated how powerful public trends could be. Once the weather improved, he would have more time to work on the farm because he didn't have to take products to town. People would come to him.

He now sold fresh eggs, fresh vegetables and herbs, along with bales of pine straw for use in landscaping. That is how he got the idea to start growing ornamental trees and bushes to expand on the concerns people had with maintaining their yards. He had more pine straw than anyone would need from the Christmas trees already, but he had never grown anything strictly for decoration. This required some study, and he had been researching the best plants and placement for landscaping yards. He could do that work himself, but not alone. He'd have to hire help to set out the plants once he sold someone on his landscaping designs. That was the only part that held back his plan.

Bryan wanted the business to grow. He wanted to capitalize on the current trends that brought people back to nature, but he had always done everything alone and on his own. He wasn't sure he wanted to be anyone else's boss.

He had a trip to town planned this afternoon to take herbs into the Ole' Thyme Italian Restaurant and Ivy's Oils & Organics. Denise Ivy was selling some of his small potted mints in her store on consignment. She was new in business and she was struggling so he hadn't asked her to buy them. She took care of them and he swapped them out regularly to make sure they always looked fresh. He had hoped her business would prosper and he might be able to introduce other products for sale there so he could expand his sales, but it was too soon to know yet. She did have a business that could blend well with his and he had considered offering her space in his as well. He didn't know if he could collaborate with someone else though.

§

Just as Cora and Conrad crossed the street, Saucy came out of the Fennel Street Bakery and started walking toward Ivy's Oils & Organics. Conrad guessed he planned to return once the stranger left just as they had so he called out a greeting to him and they waited for him to approach.

"Hey, Saucy. How are you?"

"Doing great, Chief, Mayor. Getting some exercise to walk off the banana muffin I just ate at the bakery."

"Well, we are getting ready to go into Ivy's. Want to join us?" Cora stretched out her arm towards the door to invite him.

Saucy seemed stymied by this and unsure what the right answer was. "Sure, I'll join you," he stammered. "What are we shopping for today?"

"Cora has a gift she's looking for and I'm just along for the ride," Conrad said patting Saucy on the back as he took up the rear when they walked through the door. "I don't know that I've been in here since she opened."

Denise turned at the counter in surprise when the bell over the door rang and they all walked in. She walked around the counter and pushed her long blonde hair back nervously. "Wow, I'm honored," she chirped in delight. "The Mayor and the Police Chief, both in my little old store. I couldn't be prouder. Mr. Salzman, did you bring me new customers? What can I help you with today?"

Conrad looked to Cora to signal her to take over. "Oh, this is a lovely place you have here. I'm looking for a gift for a dear friend and I wanted to look around some. I don't know what I want to get her. She just has everything, and I'm looking for inspiration." Denise thanked her and took Cora's arm to begin explaining her product offerings.

Conrad looked at Saucy curiously. "Do you have any idea what you actually do with these things in here?"

Rather than a smile or smirk as Conrad had expected, Saucy responded with sincerity. "Actually, I do know a bit about essential oils. I use them for my old man aches and find them quite helpful."

Conrad raised his eyebrows. "Really? I didn't know they helped with things like that."

"Oh, they can be used for many things. They can work on muscle pain, skin problems, breathing or digestive problems, colds and some of them just smell good. Lots of people use them to make bath stuff and candles, too."

"Do you rub it on you?" Conrad was truly bewildered by more than the information. He was dumbfounded that Saucy knew this.

"Some you apply to your skin, some can be ingested or breathed in with an air diffuser. See over here," Saucy said pulling Conrad to the side counter. "This sends a mist into the air and there is oil in the water. That way you can breathe in the benefits or just enjoy the smell."

"You have one of these things?" Conrad asked.

"I do, but it's mostly just for the scent. Some of these are very relaxing. I use vetiver and chamomile in my diffuser when I sleep. For my joint pain, I use the peppermint or wintergreen mixed with marjoram and rub it in. It helps relax the muscles."

"Well, I'll be." Conrad just shook his head in disbelief. "Maybe I need to try some."

Hearing that, Denise pivoted quickly towards Conrad. "Do you have muscle pain, Chief? Or sleep problems? Or headaches?" Before Conrad could sort out the options, Denise held up a finger and squinted both her eyes. "I bet you could use something to keep you sharp at your job."

"Oh, I could use that too," Cora said chuckling and holding up her hand.

"I have just the thing for you!" Denise went to the counter and pulled up a small bottle, opening it to hold up to Conrad's face. "Cypress is just one of many that help clear and calm your mind. You can put it in a diffuser to scent a room, rub a small dot into your wrist or just open the bottle and breathe deeply a few times a day. It has a wonderful manly scent." Denise was beaming. She loved showing off her products.

"What about me?" Cora said in a lilting voice. "My mind is far from clear most of the time." She was relieved that this brought a smile to everyone's face.

"For you, I would recommend Rosemary and Lemon mixed together. It not only helps clear your mind, but it also helps with memory recall and battling stress."

"Well, I should spray that all over City Hall," Cora said with glee. She could just imagine everyone's reaction. "Seriously though, that sounds like it would make a lovely gift for my friend. Surely, she doesn't have one already. I'll take one of those machines over there and whatever oils you think are nice. Does it come with instructions and everything so she'll know what to do with it?"

"Definitely," Denise exclaimed. "I even have several recipes for making household products from the oils that I'll include."

The ladies walked back to the counter and Cora waited while Denise gathered everything together for her.

"Chief, you really should give them a try." Saucy offered another sample bottle for him to smell. "They really are helpful and pleasant to have around."

"I think the PD would be a bit put off if I scented up the place—Not that it couldn't use a whiff of something besides leather and sweat," Conrad said smiling.

Cora joined them with her bag in hand and Conrad opened the door. "You coming, Saucy?"

"No thanks, Chief. I think I'll look around a bit."

"All-righty then, see you folks later," Conrad said as he and Cora went through the door.

"Well, that was something," Conrad said grinning. "Whatcha got in that bag?"

"I'm not really sure, but Amanda will sort it all out. It smells lovely and I'm sure Denise can use a sale. Here, can you hold this a second?" Cora pushed the bag into Conrad's arms as she dug down into the contents and extracted a small bottle. Thrusting it at Conrad in exchange for the bag she said, "This is for you."

"Well, I'll be." Conrad sniffed the bottle. "Smells like an evergreen forest."

"Sniff on that a while and see if your mind clears up. If it does, let me know. I might need a bottle for everyone on the City Council." Cora crinkled up her eyes when she grinned.

Sheri Richey

Chapter Eight

Once Denise saw that the chief and the mayor had walked by, she turned on Saucy. "Harvey, what are you doing here?"

"Hey, I'm trying to help you. I brought you customers, didn't I?"

"Okay, yes, you're right," Denise conceded, but looked skeptical. "Is there something else you wanted?"

"A couple of things, actually." Saucy walked over to the counter. "I'd like to know when I can have my garage back and I had some things I wanted to share with you. I've been doing a little research."

"I need just another week or so to get my supplies out of your garage. I've ordered bottles and labels but they aren't here yet. I'll get to them as soon as they arrive."

"I appreciate it," Saucy said. "I don't like to shovel snow and I like to put my truck up at night."

"I understand and I'll take care of it as soon as I can. What are you researching?"

"Well, I was thinking on what you could do to boost your business some and I've got a few ideas if you want to hear them."

"Sure," Denise said. "As long as it doesn't cost any money. I'm plum out of that."

"No, just some effort and some ink. You know those recipes you have. I was thinking maybe you could print up some of the ones with the yoga mat cleaners on it with your business card at the bottom and go by the gym with them. Ask them if you can leave your card at their door or counter. People would pick it up for the free recipe and your business information would lead them here to buy the stuff to make it." Denise furrowed her brow in doubt but Saucy continued. "You could do the same thing with that face scrub or moisturizer recipe and take it down to Louise's beauty shop. She'd probably let you leave some at her counter as long as she didn't sell those same products."

"Harvey, that's actually a good idea!" Denise's face glowed with creative thoughts. "I have a recipe for cuticle cream too and I could take that to the nail salon."

"There you go." Saucy smiled with satisfaction just as the chime above the door jingled.

"I can't believe you thought of that."

"You said that already," Saucy grumbled.

"Hi, Bryan," Denise said as Bryan entered with a box in his hands and Saucy nodded hello.

"Just came to check on my wee little mints and see if you wanted to add a few herbs." Bryan lifted the box lid to reveal small fairy plants of sage, spearmint and lemongrass.

"Oh, those are adorable! Yes, I'd love to put those around the store."

"These little plants are yours?" Saucy held up the small sage and touched the velvety leaf.

"Bryan has these here on consignment. Somewhere warm to show them off during the winter. I've sold a few of them," she said digging in a drawer under the counter to get out her notebook where she kept track of his payment. "Aren't they adorable?"

"Yeah?" Saucy said frowning. "But what exactly do you do with them?"

"Most people just keep them as plants, but you can use them to cook with. They're herbs, just like the dried bottled stuff you buy at the store, but better."

"Well, that's interesting," Saucy said. "I didn't know you could cook with plants like this. Maybe I should get one for June."

"You should find some recipes that show fresh spice in them and include them with the plants," Denise said. "I do that with my oils and people sometimes need a little help to understand what to do with things before they know they want to. Print out a small stack and we can sit them underneath each plant."

"Good idea," Bryan said. "I'll look into that and put something together for next time. Thanks."

"You're welcome," Denise said and then looked at Saucy. "It was actually Mr. Salzman's idea, but it's a good one. I forget people just aren't familiar with a lot of my stuff either."

"I was going to ask if you're interested in expanding a little," Bryan said cautiously. "I have some herbs drying now that I plan to bottle. In the late summer there will be preserves, too. Do you think you'd want to display any of that kind of thing?"

"I'd love the herbs," Denise said, "but I don't know about the preserves. I'd have to check with City Hall and make sure I can sell edibles with my business license."

"I didn't think about that. I'm in the county, so I don't have those restrictions. You let me know if you're interested. It will be a few months before those are ready anyway."

"Okay, Bryan. Thanks," Denise said as the door jingled on his exit.

"So, you don't buy these things from him?"

"No, I can't afford to invest in anymore overhead. He just puts them here on consignment. If they sell, I pay him a percentage of the sale. It works well for me. They're cute and add to the earthy natural look of the store I think. I'd buy them if I could. It helps him out too because during the winter, he doesn't get any traffic out his way."

"Yes, it was an excellent idea," Saucy agreed. "How did you meet Bryan? I don't really know him but I knew his dad. I know he runs the tree farm north of town."

"He just came in here one day after I opened and asked." Denise shrugged her shoulders. "I drove out and checked out his place first before I answered him. He's got a nice little business and a huge greenhouse. He showed me the plants and other things he has planned. It's a nice place and everything is organic."

"At least it's authentic," Saucy said with a disapproving scowl, which she ignored.

"I don't want any lip from you, Harvey. You're not perfect either, don't forget." Saucy made no further comments but gathered up the bottles he had removed for the Chief and put them back into their proper place.

"Bryan left his money," Denise exclaimed. "Is his truck still out there?" Running to the front window, she spotted him standing in the open door of the truck putting boxes in the extended cab. "Let me catch him," she yelled to Saucy as she ran out the door.

Denise yelled his name twice before he leaned back and she ran across the street to his truck. "Here's your money. You forgot it on the counter."

Bryan thanked her and Denise quickly ran inside rubbing her arms briskly from the cold.

"I'll get out of your hair," Saucy said as he moved toward the door. "Let me know when you need me to move some stuff over here."

"I will. Thank you, Harvey."

Saucy nodded with self-satisfaction and pulled the door shut to head down the street to his truck. He was parked in the middle of the next block and passed Amanda Morgan on his way.

"Ms. Morgan," Saucy said with a nodding smile.

"Hello, Mr. Salzman," Amanda said in return. Then she walked briskly across the street to the Caraway Café.

Chapter Nine

Amanda glanced across the street once Saucy passed by and saw Bryan driving away. She didn't look in his direction and hoped he hadn't noticed her. She had spotted him at his truck when she approached and had intentionally walked on the opposite side of the street. She wasn't ready to run into him yet. She still felt unsettled about their evening.

Seeing Denise Ivy run out to him was curious. She couldn't imagine what the two would be doing together, unless of course Bryan was dating her, too. They were about the same age she guessed. She didn't know Denise. She wasn't from Spicetown, but maybe Bryan had taken her to lunch. Maybe he just tried out several girls to see what he liked, and that's why he took her home early. She might never hear from him again.

It would make seeing him at City Hall uncomfortable though. He came in every few weeks and if it snowed heavily, she saw him more often than that. She could stay in her office, out of the lobby, if that's what she needed to do. It was really disappointing though. She had liked him. He was quietly handsome with dark hair and light gray eyes. Even though she hadn't let him talk much at dinner, when he had the chance, he was thoughtful and kind. At one point when they were out waiting on the fireworks he had begun telling her about his business expansion this spring. She had seen a light in his eyes and an eagerness that made his plans exciting. They were interrupted by one of her old high school friends and never finished the conversation.

She hadn't been to the tree farm, but the greenhouse and all the natural products he was making sounded intriguing. She always tried to eat healthy foods, regularly went to a yoga class and loved the outdoors. He had said he wanted to offer food items, too, like jams and breads. His whole demeanor had changed when he began telling her his plans and then her friend had to ruin it.

It made her realize even more that their evening could have been so much richer if she would have just stopped talking and she regretted the missed opportunity.

Amanda glanced in Ivy's Oils & Organics as she passed the door. Denise was at the counter talking on the phone. No one was in the store shopping and she hesitated but kept walking. She wanted to go in and look around, but it was too obvious. She couldn't do that today.

§

When Amanda returned to the office with her sandwich, a large brown paper bag with cord handles was sitting on her desk and Ivy's Oils & Organics was scripted across the side of the bag. She was staring at it stunned when Cora swept in the door behind her.

"Mandy, there you are. I didn't realize you were out getting lunch. I was just looking for you." Cora walked through the office and into her own, leaving Amanda standing with sandwich in hand, waiting for an explanation for the bag on her desk.

"Garrett brought this list by of things they will need for the coming year and I need you to dig up some prices for me." Cora shuffled papers around on her desk as Amanda stood in her doorway still holding her lunch bag. "Where did I put it? It has a few items that are new and so he doesn't have amounts on them. I'll need to know since it might affect the budget entries. Oh, here it is," Cora said thrusting it in Amanda's direction.

"Do you know where the bag came from?" Amanda asked quietly as she leaned forward to accept the forms.

"The bag?" Cora said puzzled at first. "Oh, the bag from Ivy's, yes. I picked that up at lunch. Can you see if you can put it together and get it working for me? Set it up somewhere in here. It's not urgent or anything. I just thought I'd give it a try. It's one of those aromatic things that makes the place smell good."

"Oh, sure," Amanda said relieved. She'd been afraid it had something to do with Bryan. "Do you mean an oil diffuser? Does it have essential oils with it?"

"Yes, that's it. It comes with oils and I guess you mix them or put water in it or something," Cora said waving her hands in the air in confusion.

"Yes. I have one at home, too. I'll set it up for you."

"Perfect. I knew you'd know what to do. No hurry though." Cora sat behind her desk lifting her reading glasses. "Oh, and I saw Chief Harris, so that's taken care of now, too. Did you need something?" Cora looked confused for a moment.

"No. No, everything is fine. I'll get right on this," Amanda said as she turned towards the door. "Did you see Bryan at Ivy's?"

"Why, no dear. Why would he be there?"

"Oh, I don't know. I thought he was there when I went to get my lunch. I thought maybe you had run into him."

"No, I just saw Saucy. He uses these oils and such. Can you imagine? He said they help with pain or something. He was the only one there when I left."

"Okay," Amanda said as she left and pulled Cora's door shut. Amanda pulled the items out of the bag, eager to see what Denise Ivy had sold to Cora. She had a number of oils at home that she ordered online. She'd learned about the use of oils when she was in college.

In her freshman year she had a roommate, Roxanne, who knew all about them. Roxanne had taken her to yoga classes, told her about meditation and was a vegetarian. Amanda had learned all about a culture completely foreign to her that first year. Growing up in Spicetown had been limiting, she'd quickly found out. She didn't endorse all of Roxanne's lifestyle choices, but it was an educational year for her and she did choose to make some changes from what she learned.

One of them was the essential oils. Roxanne taught her a lot about them, and soon she grew to love the constant fragrance. It would be nice having them at work if Cora enjoyed them. Maybe she could bring some of her own too. After all, her parents had learned to like the oils.

Unpacking the diffuser, she saw it was a quality machine that would run several hours. The oils were a brand she did not have experience with but she was pleased to see lavender included in the set and thought she would start with that.

Setting everything up, she turned it on and let it run hoping Cora would find it soothing.

§

Conrad walked in the side door of the PD and heard voices tinged with accusations raised to unnecessary levels. "What's going on in here?"

"I tried to run a plate, and she tells me it doesn't exist." Officer Roy Asher pointed a finger at Georgia in the dispatch booth. "I was looking right at it!"

Georgia looked at Conrad and rolled her eyes. "Chief, it comes up not found. That's all I can tell you. I tried it twice."

"And I suppose you couldn't have made a mistake?" Conrad said lifting his eyebrows at Roy.

"No. I was looking right at it and read it to her twice."

"Maybe it was altered," Conrad said. "Were you standing up on it or looking from your car?"

"I was in the car, but I was parked, not driving by." Roy calmed and appeared to be giving the thought consideration. "I was about fifteen feet away. It might have been taped or painted. I was too far away to see the impression."

"Well, where is the car now?" Conrad knew the answer. It was gone. Roy got so caught up in arguing with Georgia that he lost sight of what mattered. It wasn't the first time. He could be a little hot-headed.

"It's a truck. It was parked on Fennel Street. I can go take a drive back and see if it's still there."

"You do that." Conrad turned on his heels to head back to his office. Sometimes they all acted like children.

"Chief," Georgia said before he reached his office and Conrad turned back. "The Sheriff called while you were out. Said it wasn't urgent, but he'd like to talk to you when you got back."

"Okay, thanks Georgie. I'll give him a call."

Conrad shut his office door and headed for the coffee machine. He needed to relax before he made that call. Everyone said coffee was a stimulant, but for Conrad, it brought him peace. He filled it with water and sat down waiting for the gurgling sound to begin. Mixing his creamer and breathing deeply, he made the dreaded call.

"Hello, Sheriff. They tell me you called earlier?"

"Hey, Connie. I just wanted to bring you up to speed and get your help on something."

The second part of that sentence was the real reason for the contact. Bobby Bell was sharing only to trade. "Sure. What can I do for you?"

"Well, the fireworks still haven't been recovered, but that flatbed you found off Eagle Bay Road, it was the bed they were on. Somebody took them and ditched the trailer."

Conrad grunted acknowledgment. He would have preferred to hear they were still on the trailer and ruined by water. This meant someone still had possession, but he was surprised Bobby acknowledged that he found the trailer. He expected the young officer would tell him of their talk, but also for Bobby to take credit. He knew better than to let down his guard and think Bobby had evolved into a decent trustworthy person. He was probably being set up for something.

"We don't know anything more than the white truck sighting I told you about before, but I wanted you to know they are still missing in case you run across something or hear something," Sheriff Bell chuckled. "It's a big wide load so if they catch a flame, it's going to sound like World War III. It's not the kind of stuff people shoot off in the backyard, you know."

"Yes, I understand."

"So, let me know—Let your guys know. They may have been carted off and sold elsewhere, but I'd hate someone to get hurt not knowing what they were messing with."

"Yes, you're right. That could be dangerous. I appreciate the heads-up." Conrad ended the call. He would relay this to Wink when he arrived later this afternoon. Conrad couldn't help thinking about Saucy's truck sitting outside the garage instead of secured away. Saucy had always put his truck up at night. Something was in his garage and Conrad hoped it wasn't fireworks.

Conrad rose from his desk and opened his office door. He hated being closed in and only did it when he needed privacy. When he opened the door, he could hear Georgia talking to another officer about Roy and went back out to dispatch to find out about the bad plates.

"Did you hear back from Roy?"

"Yes, but the truck's gone," Georgia said shaking her head in disappointment. "You know if he didn't think he was always right about everything—" Georgia's complaint was cut short by Roy's voice on the radio advising he was returning to the station.

"I know," Conrad said nodding and waving the notion away in hopes of placating Georgia before she continued her rant. "You said it was a truck?"

"Yeah, a white Dodge Ram, all beat up, he thinks about a '98," Georgia said before she turned to answer an incoming phone call.

"Have Roy come see me when he comes in," Conrad told the others in the room as he walked back to his office. He needed to know why Roy was running these plates.

Sheri Richey

Chapter Ten

"Oh, Mandy," Cora said breathing deeply as she walked out of her office and into Amanda's. "That smells lovely. I could get used to this." Amanda's face beamed.

"I'd hoped you would like it because I have lots of these at home. We could try a different scent every day or combine some that you like. I enjoy it, too. It's relaxing."

"I'm going to leave my door open so it comes in here more."

"I can move the machine in there for you," Amanda offered as she rose from her seat.

"Oh no, dear. That's okay. I could smell it even with my door shut. This is a good place for both of us and maybe it can reach the lobby a bit from here, too." Cora turned to go back through her open door and then paused. "You asked about seeing Bryan earlier? Did you talk to him at lunch?"

"No, I just thought I saw him drive by as I was walking to the Caraway. It looked like he walked out of Ivy's Oils and then drove down the street. I thought maybe you were in there then."

"Oh, I see. I guess you haven't heard from him?" Amanda shook her head no. "It's early yet and I don't think he'll be in the office until next Friday, unless something comes up before then." Cora saw Amanda's eyes dart toward the door to the lobby as she kept an eye on who came and went regularly. "You'll probably hear from him soon," Cora added in solace.

"I don't know," Amanda said pensively. "Maybe he's dating the lady that runs Ivy's. I can't imagine what business he would have in there otherwise. He might date around town and I just didn't realize it. I don't know Denise Ivy, but I guess she's single and about his age."

"Well, maybe, but I don't really see that," Cora said frowning. "Bryan doesn't seem like that type." Cora wasn't sure what type that was, but from what she'd recently seen, he seemed too shy and quiet to be a player. Perhaps Amanda was just trying to paint Bryan in an undesirable light to lessen the disappointment if he never called.

"I'll see what I can find out about it though." Cora ambled back into her office. If Bryan was that type of young man, the women of Spicetown would know and they would talk.

"Oh, Amanda, would you please check with your mom and see if she can put me down in her crowded book? I could use a touch-up." Cora winked and patted the back of her head to lighten the mood.

Amanda's mother, Louise Morgan, ran the local beauty shop and Cora had her hair done there every month. She had a coppery ginger color, and the roots had to be touched up every three to four weeks. She joked about it openly as her hair would be snow white otherwise, but she always used color to match as closely as she could to the color of her youth. It was the color of her hair that Bing always said made her stand out like a shiny penny and she wasn't going to let age take that away.

"Will do," Amanda said cheerfully, clearly forgetting the gloom of Bryan.

§

Conrad looked up when he heard boots shuffling towards his office door and saw Roy standing on the threshold. "You wanted to see me, Chief?" Roy had lost his bravado and seemed mildly sheepish as Conrad motioned him in the door.

"Have a seat," Conrad said as he stood to freshen his coffee. "Tell me about this truck you saw today, the white one."

"Oh, yeah it was just a beat up older Dodge Ram parked near the Fennel Street Bakery, but the guy getting out of it was a squirrelly looking little dude I've never seen before. I was just running the plates to see if he was from around these parts."

"So, he didn't commit any offense, driving or otherwise," Conrad mused but Roy sat up straighter prepared to defend his actions. Conrad saw by his demeanor that he thought his judgment was in question. "Nothing wrong with checking, but tell me, what did he look like?"

Roy dropped into a chair across from Conrad's desk and his posture relaxed. "Well, he was just a creepy little guy. Probably didn't weigh more than 140, about 5'5, black stringy hair and dressed all in black. It wasn't just his clothes though," Roy said, struggling to describe the vibe he felt upon seeing the driver. "He just seemed like he was up to no good. You know what I mean? He just--"

"I think I saw him, too," Conrad said. "He did have an unscrupulous look about him. I wondered who he was. I was eating in the Caraway Cafe and saw him walk by. I didn't see the truck though."

"Well, I'm sorry I didn't get the plate. I just never thought it was doctored up. I was hoping to find out where he came from and who he was," Roy said dropping his chin down towards his chest to avoid Conrad's gaze as he returned to his desk with fresh coffee.

"I guess Wink told you about the fireworks on New Year's?"

"Yeah, I wasn't working, but he told me the next day."

"They don't have much to go on, but they had one witness mention a white truck. No other details, but of course, it was dark and just driving by, but they are hoping we will keep our eyes peeled."

"Oh, sure thing, Chief," Roy grunted as he scooted forward to rise from the chair. Roy was a big man and carried most of it in his gut. "If I see it again, I'll get a better look at those plates for you."

"Thanks, Roy," Conrad said to his back as he walked to the door. "Oh, and Roy?" Roy stopped in the doorway and turned back. "Go easy on Georgie, will you?"

"Oh, sure, sure," Roy held up his hand to show he meant no harm and because he couldn't really defend his actions otherwise.

"What was the tag you ran?" Conrad asked as Roy started to go around the corner of the door.

"Oh, I thought it was Papa-Oscar-Yankee-5718." Conrad just nodded and waved him on. He had an idea. It might be a long shot, but he wanted to look at that tag number a bit and see what he could make of it.

Conrad began running plates with changes he thought could be done easily. If white tape was used, that plate could have read a B instead of a P, so he checked on that number. The 7 could have been a Z or the 8 a 3, so he tried all of those combinations singly and together. After exhausting all possibilities that he could imagine, he switched to the opposite tactic. If black tape was used, the O could have been a C and the 8" could have been a 6. If the guy had been really industrious, he could have used both.

When he looked up to find Wink in his doorway and the sun beginning to set, he knew he had been playing with combinations a lot longer than he thought.

"Hey, boss." Wink put his hand on the back of the chair facing Conrad's desk. "You busy?"

"No, have a seat. I need to talk to you," Conrad pushed the laptop screen away and rubbed his eyes. "I talked to the sheriff today."

"Yeah? What did he have to say?"

"Well, turns out that the trailer in the lake was the right one, but the goods were gone." Conrad held his hands out with his palms up to show defeat. "It would have been so nice if they had pulled out wet ruined crates of fireworks when the trailer was pulled out of the lake."

"So, do they have anything more? You found the trailer. What have their fancy detectives found?"

"He didn't have anything to add. They are still looking for a white truck. They don't have anything that he shared."

"There are a million white trucks and driving down Eagle Bay, doesn't mean much." Wink rolled his eyes.

"I know, but assuming the white truck angle might be something. There was one in town today that wasn't a Spicetown regular. I think I've narrowed it down and if so, it's a less than desirable visitor. Do you know a Shawn Ellis from Paxton?"

"No," Wink said shaking his head. "He was in town today?"

"Yes, I saw a stranger walking on Fennel Street and watched him go into Ivy's Oils & Organics. He was there a while, and I checked on Denise after, but she didn't mention him. Later, Roy tried to run plates on a white truck that I think is the same guy and the run failed, so I've been playing with numbers to see if I could figure it out."

"Roy screw up the number?" Wink wrinkled his brow.

"I don't think so." Conrad leaned back in his chair and took a deep breath. "I think the tags were doctored. They don't come back at all."

"So, is the truck stolen?"

"No. Roy gave Georgie Papa-Oscar-Yankee 5718, and it doesn't come back. But Papa-Charlie-Yankee 5716 hits on Shawn Ellis from Paxton with a white truck and the photo looks like the guy I saw. I'm waiting for Roy to come in and see if it's the same guy he saw. Maybe it's nothing," Conrad said shrugging.

"You don't tamper with tags for no reason," Wink mused.

"True, but the guy has a sheet, so it could be anything."

"Has he done time?" Wink asked.

"Three years for felony theft and a bunch of smaller stuff. He's been out a couple of years though." Conrad shrugged. He didn't really know what to do with this information other than be suspicious of the guy in general. Ellis hadn't done anything that he could see, other than tamper with his vehicle tag. Even if he was bad news, nothing tied him to the fireworks except a white truck, which was nothing.

"Fireworks or not, we don't want him in Spicetown," Wink barked out. Conrad smiled because that was it in a nutshell. "I'll keep an eye out though. Nothing else, we'll get him for messing with the tags." Wink smirked and pushed the chair back just as the side door opened and Roy came down the hall.

"Hey, Roy," Conrad yelled as he walked by. "Come look at this picture."

Roy walked around the side of the desk as Conrad shifted the laptop. "Yep, that's him. He looks like a weasel. How did you find him?"

"I saw him earlier, too, and I played around with the tags. He's altered them a little. Pull him if you see him again though. Get him on the tags," Conrad said as Roy nodded.

"He best stay out of Spicetown," Roy huffed as he pulled up his waistband partially over his stomach. The belt always slipped down under and disappeared.

"I'll send out his sheet to everybody. If he comes back to town, we'll fix those plates for him," Wink assured Conrad as he and Roy walked out of Conrad's office.

Chapter Eleven

Amanda tapped on the mayor's door lightly as it was already ajar. "Mayor?"

"Yes. Come in, Mandy. I know you're going to tell me I need to get out of here and you're right," Cora said straightening things on her desk and putting her laptop to sleep. "I'm going to be late."

Amanda nodded her head forcefully which made her shoulder length ash blonde hair swing as she went back to her desk. Relieved Cora was on her way out, she looked up when she came bustling through the doorway. "Don't worry. Mom won't turn you away if you're late." Amanda smiled. She'd told Cora her hair appointment was fifteen minutes earlier than it was because she knew getting Cora out the door in the middle of the afternoon was difficult.

"I need some exercise anyway. I'll just run." Cora winked at Amanda as she scurried down the back hall to get her coat. Amanda smiled and rolled her eyes once Cora was out of her sight.

Cora did try to walk deliberately down the sidewalk which was her version of running and limited her looking around. She was usually a casual stroller because she wanted to see everything and everybody around her, but there was no time for that today. Once she made the corner on Clove Street, she almost bumped into Harvey Salzman turning onto Clove Street from the alley.

"Afternoon, Mayor," Saucy said, nodding his head in greeting. "In a hurry?"

"Oh dear, yes," Cora said smiling, pleased that her purposeful stride was apparent. "I have an appointment and I'm late."

"Okay. I won't delay you. You have a good day," Saucy said as he smiled back as he passed.

"Thank you. You, too." Cora waved without any hesitation in her step.

She reached the door to Louise Morgan's beauty shop and took a deep breath before turning the knob. She steadied herself a moment to disguise her breathlessness.

Louise had run this beauty shop all her life. She didn't care for fancy names or spices and wasn't going to join in the naming game that all the other businesses in town played. It was Louise's Beauty Salon, and that's all it had ever been. She survived a block off the main street by maintaining long-time customers and having the best prom up-do in town.

Cora had been going there since she first started teaching school. Louise had been the first and only one to cover her gray and help her keep her girlish copper color intact. There were many other women in town that had gone to Louise for decades, too, and they brought in their daughters and grandchildren. The place was always packed despite the fly-by-night quick-cut shops that popped up to compete with her.

The bell jingled over Cora's head as she walked into the warmth of the shop. The chemical smells of permanent solutions and heated irons wafted over her. She was ready for some pampering.

All the ladies welcomed her as she removed her coat, tugged on her skirt that had ridden up during her boisterous walk and glanced around the room. Some with rollers in their hair, some in chairs with wet heads and others with plastic bags or foil wrapped around their hair. They were all chattering loudly to be heard over the dryers with towels clipped over their shoulders.

"Hello, everyone." Cora waved and found a chair to sit down. It was busier than usual so she hoped her late arrival wouldn't have been noticed at all.

"Mayor? If you'd like to follow me, I'll go ahead and shampoo you. Louise will be ready for you soon." Cora looked up blankly for a moment. She didn't think she knew this young woman.

"Tara? Is that you?" Cora beamed once she recognized her as a former student.

"Yes, it's me," Tara said meekly with a flush to her face. Pale and thin with pink hair now, Tara had been a chubby be-spectacled quiet child.

"I didn't know you were working here." Cora followed Tara to the shampoo bowls.

"I started in October," Tara said as she draped a plastic cape across the front of Cora and released the chair to lower her back to the bowl.

"I guessed I've just missed you when I've been in here."

Cora relaxed and shut her eyes. She enjoyed the feel of the warm water and the lather working through her hair. It was one of those rare moments when all her plans and lists completely left her mind. Perhaps the permanent solution worked like the aromatic essential oils. She thought of nothing but the soothing massage and the comforting scents—and then Saucy.

Why Saucy would be coming out of the alley? There was nothing down there and no parking spaces either. It was rather odd. She couldn't imagine where he'd been or why he'd been there. There must be more to that man than she knew.

Returning her to an up-right position, Tara wrapped a towel around Cora's head and directed her to her seat in the front of the salon to wait for Louise.

"What have you heard about that, Cora?" Louise hollered over the hair dryer running beside her and Cora's head jerked around.

"What? Heard about what?"

"The fireworks thing," Louise yelled. "What happened New Year's Eve?"

"Oh, I haven't heard anything," Cora said dismissively. "Just whatever is in the papers."

"I heard somebody stole them," Karen Goldman said from three chairs down. "I think they stole them right out from under the sheriff's nose."

"Really?" Darlene Kendall leaned forward and looked at Cora. "We should have just done our own. Don't you think so, Mayor?"

"It was unfortunate," Cora said, wishing the topic away, "But things happen sometimes..."

"Chief Connie never would have let that happen," Karen Goldman said indignantly. Karen was fiercely loyal to Conrad Harris for finding her seven-year-old son when he bicycled away too far one day. She had called him in terror and Conrad had driven around until he found him playing several blocks away. Too far for him to have gone, but in no danger. Karen told the story all over town repeatedly.

"Did everyone have a nice holiday otherwise?" Cora interjected, hoping to move to another topic.

"My Jeffrey was home for Christmas," Darlene's eyes darted towards Tara at the front desk writing in the appointment book with the phone pinched between her shoulder and her ear. Jeffrey was Darlene's youngest son who was away at college.

"He called on Miss Tara over there," Darlene said pointing, "and they got together." Her mischievous smile relayed her wishful thinking. She wanted her son to come home after he graduated and settle down in Spicetown. Her other children had grown up and moved away.

"Well, my Amanda had a New Year's date with Bryan Stotlar," Louise said with a tone of disbelief.

"Really?" Darlene said. "How did that go?"

"I don't know. She never tells me anything," Louise said looking at Cora. "How did it go, Cora?" When all eyes turned to Cora, she was mildly flustered.

"I think it went fine," Cora stammered. "I mean the fireworks were a disappointment, but I guess it went fine." Cora couldn't help it if Louise had failed to keep her daughter's confidences and Amanda refused to tell her anything personal anymore. She didn't want to be in the middle of them.

"He seems like a nice guy," Karen said. "Kind of quiet. Keeps to himself."

"Yes, but he has a nice place," Darlene interjected. "We bought our tree from him this year. He's fixed it up a lot and I think he's getting ready to do more work out there."

"Well, I don't know much about him," Louise said. "His mother used to come in here but she was Sharon's customer. She seemed nice, but I never talked to her much."

"Amanda's doing a wonderful job at City Hall." Cora hoped to turn the conversation around. "You should be very proud of her."

"Oh, I am." Louise swept the cape off Darlene's shoulders and spraying the back of her hair with hair spray. "She loves working up there."

Darlene and Louise finished their business and Darlene walked toward the counter to pay just as Louise motioned for Cora to come to her chair.

"It was nice to see you, Mayor," Darlene called out from the door. "You take care."

"Thank you," Cora said waving. "You, too."

Louise spun Cora around until she was facing the mirror and began to pull the comb through her hair roughly. "So, color today? A little trim?"

"Yes, please." Cora sat back in the chair as Louise went to the back for the color.

"You know," Karen Goldman said leaning forward to catch Cora's attention. "I heard Bryan Stotlar is doing some business with Denise Ivy in that organic oil place." She nodded as if she was insinuating something unscrupulous was afoot.

"I hadn't heard that," Cora said innocently. "I was in Ivy's Oils & Organics just the other day. It's an interesting place."

"I haven't been, but I hear Bryan's selling some stuff or she's selling some of his stuff in the store now," Karen said sitting back in her chair as Louise approached.

"Maybe he enjoys the oils," Cora said smiling. "You'd be surprised. A lot people have started trying them nowadays."

"Trying what?" Louise said as she returned and began sectioning Cora's hair with her comb.

"Essential oils," Cora said, thinking again of Saucy.

"Oh, Amanda loves that stuff. She's always got something shooting out of that machine of hers. I never know what my house will smell like from one day to the next." Louise was always gruff in her exterior approach, but Cora could tell by her smirk that she enjoyed the oils too.

"Yes, we have them at the office now and I'm enjoying it." Cora turned her eyes to Karen. Louise was holding her hair so she couldn't turn her head.

"You should go up to Ivy's and look around. It's a cute place." Cora preferred to encourage local business rather than local gossip. "Bryan runs a snowplow for the city, so we see him occasionally, too. I don't know much about his tree business though."

"I hear he's getting into that organic stuff now, so he's selling something there that he grows. I don't really know what, but he's supposed to be into that now, too." Karen busied herself in the mirror and shut her eyes tightly as her stylist misted a fine layer of hair spray across her bangs. "I guess that's the in thing now."

As Karen made her way to the counter, Louise looked at Cora through the mirror. "So, what do you know about this guy? Is he okay? He's older, isn't he?"

Cora knew she was asking if she should approve of Amanda dating Bryan and Cora wasn't sure of that herself. "I don't know him well, Louise. He's not chatty when he's in the office so I couldn't say one way or the other. Amanda seems to like him." That was as far as Cora would go. She didn't want Louise adding her own interpretive spin to it.

"She hasn't mentioned him since New Year's so maybe it was just a onetime thing," Louise said shrugging. Cora nodded very slightly as her head movement was still limited but she had said all she was going to on the subject.

"You know," Cora said in another attempt to control the topic, "when I was walking over, I ran into Harvey Salzman."

"Saucy?" Louise said with a chuckle.

"Yes, but he was coming out of the alley between Fennel and Clove Street. I was in such a hurry, I couldn't chat, but I can't imagine why he'd be down there." Cora brought this up primarily because if something was going on, Louise would know about it. It could be dicey talking to Louise sometimes.

"I saw him drive down there last week, too. I think maybe he's working at one of those stores part-time and parking back there. I honked at him one day when I saw him pulling out. It was right after quitting time. I meant to ask his sister, June, about it when she came in."

"That would make sense," Cora said. "I just thought it odd. There's nothing much down there."

"He's pretty fond of the bakery. I've run into him in there. Maybe he's helping them out," Louise suggested and let the topic drop. Cora made a mental note to ask Conrad about it.

"How is June?" Cora asked. "I haven't seen her in a long time."

"She doesn't get out as much anymore. She's had some health problems, but she still cooks Saucy dinner every Wednesday night and tries to keep him on the straight and narrow," Louise said chuckling. "She's done that every Wednesday since Saucy's wife left."

"Well, that's nice of her," Cora said as Louise set the timer for her color and motioned for her to move to a side chair. Cora picked up a magazine and settled in to wait a bit while Louise moved a young boy into her chair for a cut just as the front door bell jingled.

"I think she's having some financial problems." Louise tossed a glance over her shoulder at Cora. "I heard she's been selling off some furniture and doing some alterations for folks. Things must be tight."

Cold air rushed into the salon and Cora saw Denise Ivy talking to Tara at the front desk. She had something in her hand she was showing to Tara as Tara nodded and smiled. When Denise turned around, Cora smiled and greeted her as Tara approached Louise. Although Tara spoke softly and tried to ask Louise a question privately, Louise didn't have a subtle response.

"What? What's this?" Louise yelled over the hair dryers and looked at Denise as she approached.

"Sorry," Denise said. "I don't mean to interrupt your work. I can come back if another time would be better."

"It's always like this," Louise snapped as she paused with the hair clippers turned off. "What can I do for you?"

"I'm Denise Ivy and I own Ivy's Oils & Organics on Fennel Street." Denise paused hoping Louise would acknowledge the store, but she said nothing. "I just wondered if I could leave a flyer on your counter about my store. It's a recipe to make a facial scrub and a coupon."

Louise frowned and didn't answer immediately, but finally nodded and turned the clippers back on. "Sure. That would be okay."

"Thank you," Denise said meekly and handed the stack to Tara. "I won't keep you. I appreciate it," she said as she waved and walked towards the door.

"I enjoyed your oils," Cora said to distract Denise from Louise's sour response. She felt sorry for Denise. Louise had not been very welcoming, and it was challenging to walk into a business of strangers and ask for their help. Louise was not easy to approach.

"Oh, good," Denise said smiling. "I'm so glad you enjoyed them. I hope you come back soon."

Cora just smiled and waved as Denise went out the door. Cora could tell marketing was a struggle for Denise. She was very engaging when she talked about the oils. It was obvious she believed strongly in their benefits and enjoyed promoting them if she had a receptive audience but approaching new people to engage with them was a chore for her.

When Cora was called back to Louise's chair, Louise talked the entire time about her oldest son. She had seen him at Christmas and her grandchildren had visited too. Cora was able to just nod and listen without any commitment. As she left the salon, she took one of Denise's ads with her.

Chapter Twelve

Bryan grabbed his jacket and ran for the front door when he heard the delivery truck honk outside. This was delivery day for all the new supplies he had ordered and his heart raced as if it was Christmas morning. Directing the driver to pull closer to the greenhouse, he unlocked and lifted the wide sliding door so the items could be moved inside easily. There were bags of soil and fertilizers, all sizes of planters, trees, seeds, tools, bare-root plants, and display stands all wrapped tightly away from the cold winter breeze.

Once the truck left, he spent the morning opening and checking all the contents. He assembled the display stands he'd place outside in spring and organized all the planters on storage racks. As he worked, his imagination was rolling everything out for spring with painted signs and the bustle of customers. It energized his mood and busied his hands until all his troubles were forgotten.

As the sun set and the temperature dropped, Bryan went in to scrub the dirt from around his fingernails and his stomach told him he had forgotten to eat all day. After looking through his pantry he filled a pot with water and turned it on to boil. Selecting ingredients for sauce, he added everything to a saucepan and pinched a few herbs to toss in.

He had developed many cooking talents in the pursuit of expanding the sale of his herbs. He was no longer lost in the kitchen and found recipes easy to follow. Over the years, he had settled on what pleased him most and was able to prepare almost all of his mother's dishes as well as she did.

He wasn't comfortable sitting in restaurants alone and he couldn't routinely tolerate fast food, so learning to cook had been a necessity and a challenge. Fortunately, it had also entertained him for several months.

Just as he was straining the water from the boiled pasta, his cell phone rang. Glancing at it, he saw it was Denise Ivy calling and he sat the hot pan in the sink to grab his phone.

"Hello?" Bryan was surprised at the call. Denise had never called him before.

"Hi, Bryan. It's Denise Ivy at the store. I hope you don't mind my calling, but there was a lady in the store today asking about your plants and I didn't know what to tell her."

"No, that's fine. What did she want to know?"

"Well, she bought what I had and said she needs six more. She asked about going out to your farm, but I told her you weren't open until March. I didn't know what to tell her."

"That's true, but if I'm here, I don't mind helping her."

"I didn't want to just give her your number without asking first. I just didn't know what to tell her. I have her phone number if you want to call her or if you want to bring in more plants, I'll call her so she can come back by."

Bryan preferred the latter option, but that wasn't very good customer service. The products were his, and it wasn't Denise's problem.

"I'll give her a call and see if I have what she's looking for. Thanks for letting me know."

Denise gave him the phone number, and he called the customer back. She wanted six more mint or sage plants, which he had, but she needed them before the weekend. He promised her he would bring them into Denise's store the following day for her so she didn't have to drive out to his place. He needed to go into town tomorrow anyway to pick up his check at City Hall. He wanted to see Amanda when he went in, but he didn't know how she would react to him. He hoped she would be friendly and not try to avoid him.

§

Walking in the office door several days later, Cora moaned as she breathed in deeply. "Hmm, it smells heavenly in here. It's almost closing time, and it's still going strong. What did you say that was again?"

"Bergamot," Amanda smiled and lifted her chin to breathe deeply. "I brought it from home."

"I love it. Can you get Vitamin C from breathing it in?"

"I don't know, but I don't think so." Amanda held up the bottle for Cora to see.

"I've never heard of it, but I like it," Cora said walking into her office to set down her stack of notes and her handbag. "The others didn't seem to last all day, but maybe it's because I've been out of the office for a bit."

Amanda walked into Cora's office and put her mail in a tray by Cora's monitor. "No, It's Ivy's oils. I tested them and they aren't pure so they just don't last as long."

"Aren't pure?" Cora said puzzled. "You mean they aren't real essential oils? How do you test them?"

"They're oily," Amanda said shrugging. "When I opened the bottles to set up the diffuser, they don't have a plastic dropper like mine and I got some on my hands. They leave an oily feeling and they shouldn't. At least most of them shouldn't. I think Ivy's oils are cut with something to dilute them and that's why they don't last as long as mine."

"Hmm," Cora said. "That's odd. The whole time I was in the shop she kept saying all of her oils were pure and organic. Doesn't the bottle say it's pure?"

"It does, but the bottles are odd, too. They're tinted like they should be but the purple labels keep coming off. I had to tape one of them to get it to stay. Maybe I got it oily with my hands when I opened it, but most essential oils aren't like that. A few are oily, but not Bergamot or Lavender."

"Well, I guess we'll need to order your kind when we run out. That's a shame." Cora sat down behind her desk. She liked to support local business, but she didn't like someone selling her inferior products and trying to deceive her. *Perhaps Denise doesn't know as much about her own products as she boasted*, she thought.

As Amanda turned to leave Cora's office, Conrad walked in. "Hi, Chief," Amanda said as she walked around him to leave the office. "You snuck up on me."

Conrad chuckled at that and patted his stomach. "I don't get away with that much anymore."

"Hey, Connie. Have a seat." Cora turned on her desk lamp to brighten things as the day was dreary and the sun setting already. "Amanda was just telling me an interesting story."

"Really? A story about what?"

"Well, you know those oils we bought last week at Ivy's? We've been running the little machine out there."

"Yeah, I can smell it. You can even smell it in the lobby."

"Today you can," Cora said, "but that's because this one is what Amanda brought from home. She said the oils Denise sold us weren't pure even though the label says they are. They're diluted with something and the ones we used last week didn't smell that strong. They didn't last all day either." Cora waited for Conrad's response but when he said nothing, she leaned forward on her elbows and peered at him. "Do you think she knows that? Do you think she's intentionally misleading people?"

"Well, I don't know," Conrad grinned impishly, "but I can tell you're irked about it."

"Yes, I am." Cora huffed. "I don't like to be taken. And I don't like to think others are either. I think I'm going down there and having a little talk with Miss Ivy."

"Now, Cora Mae. Don't go doing that just yet. Maybe it was the company, a bad bottle. Don't jump to conclusions. Let's give her another chance before we slap the cuffs on." Conrad laughed at his own jab and then saw Cora's expression. She didn't appreciate being teased.

"Maybe I'll just tell Saucy about it. Then I'll send him over to you to file a report," Cora said jabbing her finger in the air to point at Conrad. Cora said it jokingly, but she meant it. "I'll give her another chance. I'll buy another bottle and we'll see, but if it's bad too, I won't let it go unaddressed."

Conrad turned in his seat to look out the doorway towards Amanda's office. "Mandy, can you come in here?"

"Sure, Chief. How can I help you?"

"Cora's telling me about the oils. How do you know they aren't what they say they should be?"

Amanda explained her testing procedure again.

"I don't understand," Conrad said frowning. "These are oils. Shouldn't oil be oily?"

"Essential oils are a plant product and they will evaporate quickly if you put a drop on a piece of paper. If they are diluted with a carrier oil that oil will leave a spot on the paper. It won't go away. That's how my college roommate taught me to test the quality of oils I bought. She knew a lot about them. I've done it many times, and it seems to be true. My lavender disappears. Miss Ivy's lavender doesn't. Plus, we can tell a difference in how strong the smell is and how long it lasts."

"True." Cora nodded and pointed a finger at Conrad. "The reason you smelled this all the way in the lobby is because Amanda brought it from home. We've been doing this every day since the day I bought them and no one has even noticed outside of her office."

"So, it's not just one bottle? It's like this with all of them?"

"I haven't opened all of them yet," Amanda said. "I could test them all for you though."

"You do that, Mandy." Conrad lifted his foot to rest his ankle across his knee. "I'll bring mine by and you can test it, too. Then we'll see what we got."

"Ok, Chief," Amanda said as she left the office, pulling Cora's door shut behind her.

Walking back to her desk, she saw Bryan walking out the front door. He didn't look back, and he didn't see her. She knew it was pay day, and she had been watching for him all morning. Her heart sunk at the missed opportunity. Unless it snowed, she wouldn't have another chance to see him for two weeks.

"So, Connie, what brings you by?" Cora said after they decided to wait on Amanda's test results. She was going to reserve judgment for a short time.

"Just stopped in on my way out. I was here to tell Jimmy Kole about some damage to a street sign so he could get someone to check on it. I just noticed it when I was driving around today. I guess someone hit it."

"Are you doing patrol now?"

"I've been doing a little this last week or so."

"You must be looking for someone," Cora said with a suggestive lilt in her voice. Conrad didn't patrol unless he had a good reason.

"That guy I saw before we went to Ivy's last week, I've been keeping an eye out for him."

"She didn't even mention him when we were there. What is it you think he's done?"

"Roy tried to run his tags, and they were doctored up. He's not a good character, and I'd like to know what he's up to if he's here in Spicetown."

"Hmm," Cora hummed. "I wonder if Denise knows him?"

"I don't know but he drives an old white truck and we're keeping an eye out for it."

"I'll let you know if I see him," Cora said as she turned her desk lamp off.

"You do that. I'm getting a little tired of looking for white trucks." Conrad puffed. "You'd be amazed at how many there are here in town."

"That reminds me," Cora said when her mind connected to the sight of a white truck. "I saw Saucy last week, and he was coming out of the alley that runs behind Fennel Street. I was headed down Clove to go around the block to Louise's and he just walked out. I asked Louise about it. She said she saw him going back there, too. Is there something going on down that alley?"

"Not that I know about." Conrad looked up at the ceiling in thought. "It's just a through-way for the trash truck to collect behind the businesses. Not much room back there to do anything but drive through it I don't think. Maybe he's taking a shortcut?" Conrad remembered then that Wink had seen a white truck down that alley on New Year's Eve. Maybe that was Saucy, too.

"I think there's a lot more to Saucy than I know," Cora said, glancing at the clock. It was time for the City Hall doors to be locked.

"I've been thinking the same thing." Conrad rose from his chair. "I'm heading over to Ole'

Thyme Italian for something to eat. Do you want to join me?" It was time to explore a few issues he'd uncovered about Saucy and get an unbiased, civilian take on things.

"Yes, I was just thinking about that too." Cora clicked her computer mouse to log off and opened her drawer for her bag.

Chapter Thirteen

Amanda locked the City Hall doors and waited for the customers inside to complete their business so she could let them out. If she didn't do that, people would just keep coming in. She waved at Cora and Conrad as they walked out the back entrance and she watched the last visitor leave. Once the doors were locked for the final time, Amanda turned to walk back to her office and shut down her computer.

"Hey, Mandy," Laura called out from the front desk. "Did you see Bryan when he was here?"

Amanda walked over to the counter to Laura's station and saw the other girls packing up their stuff to leave. Laura was logging off her computer too. "No, I guess I missed him."

"Well, he looked in your office and asked if you were around. I didn't know where you were."

"I was probably in the mayor's office," Amanda said trying to rein in her disappointment. "He was in to pick up his check?"

"Yeah, and he asked a bunch of questions about business licenses." Laura pulled her purse from her desk drawer.

"Why? He lives in the county. He doesn't have to be licensed in Spicetown."

"I know, but he was asking about Ivy's Oils & Organics. He wanted to know if she could sell edible stuff with her license or if she had to do something special to be able to do that."

"Did he say why he was asking?" Amanda asked. *Why would Bryan care about that? Was he taking care of Denise's business now too?*

"Didn't say." Laura shrugged her shoulders. "Maybe he wants to sell more stuff there. I think he's got some stuff of his already in there. I heard him talking to Carrie about it a few weeks ago. Plants or something—I didn't really pay close attention. Didn't he mention that to you?"

"No, I don't know, maybe he did." Amanda hadn't learned much of anything about him from their date because she didn't let him talk.

"Are you guys going out again?" Laura walked around the counter.

"I don't know that either." Amanda headed back to her office to lock up as Laura called out a goodbye from the back hallway.

§

"So, let me get this straight." Cora leaned back in her chair to take a deep breath. She had eaten too much and her clothes were binding. So much for the healthy New Year, but the ravioli had been excellent. "Saucy looked you right in the eye and lied to you. I mean that's what you're saying here."

"Well, yes," Conrad said as he stirred his coffee. "He said he returned home around 7:00 after eating dinner here. It was just a few minutes before midnight and his truck hood was warm. He lied to me. I don't know if he was the one Wink saw in the alley or not."

The waitress brought Cora a small pot of hot water for her tea and she pushed her tea bag into her cup after thanking her.

"Do you think Saucy has taken a part-time job somewhere? Louise thought he might be working for one of the businesses on Fennel Street. Do the workers park back there in the alley?"

"Not usually. There's really not room. Sometimes I see a delivery truck in or out but it's not an employee parking area. I'm still stymied by the essential oil speech he gave me. I don't think we know what Saucy's up to, but he's up to something."

"Louise told me his sister, June, cooks dinner for him every Wednesday evening. They used to be estranged when Saucy was married, but they're apparently on good terms now."

"Saucy told me he always eats here every Tuesday evening. Maybe he goes out every night."

"Maybe," Cora said concentrating. "June's husband died a few years back and Louise also said June was having financial problems. She's selling furniture and doing alterations. Saucy could be trying to help June out and doesn't want anybody to know."

"I could use someone to let out my waistband about now." Conrad chuckled as he shifted his belt buckle.

Cora smiled and nodded in agreement.

"When Amanda told me about the oils being fake, my first, well— my second thought was that I should tell Saucy. He knows so much about them, but maybe he's working for Denise."

"Maybe." Conrad shook his head to let the waitress know he didn't need anything else. "But why did Denise call him Mr. Salzman when he entered that day? I remember just because it struck me oddly. It reminded me that she was new to town."

"We've covered a lot of maybes," Cora said smiling.

"Indeed, we have." Conrad stretched his back out by sitting forward in his chair as he pushed his cup away. "Maybe," Conrad said with exaggerated slowness, "we need to fill in some of these holes."

After they quarreled about the check, they left with a plan. Cora would find out if he was working somewhere. Conrad would keep an eye on his garage and his movements.

§

Throughout the week, Amanda tested all the products Cora purchased from Ivy's Oils & Organics and found only one of them to be pure. Conrad had dropped off his bottle of cypress essential oil Cora had given him that day. It had been purchased separately and was not in the boxed set she had received with the diffuser. It had a different brand on the label and it did pass her white paper purity test. She decided it was time for her to go shopping.

During her lunch hour, she walked down to pick up a sandwich and stopped in Ivy's Oils & Organics with her coupon in hand. Her mother had given her one of the coupons left at the front desk of her shop because she thought Amanda might want to shop there. She specifically wanted to see what brands Denise carried and buy a few of them to test. It was always possible that Denise didn't know what she was selling.

As the bell over the door jingled, Denise moved a box from the counter down to the floor. "Welcome to Ivy's!"

Amanda nodded and smiled. Although she had been reading up on essential oils since this issue arose, she decided in that instant to play the novice and see what Denise had to say.

"Hi," Amanda said with a meek smile. "I was hoping you could help me. I was given an oil diffuser as a gift and I need some essential oils for it."

"Oh, what a wonderful gift," Denise said enthusiastically. "I know we can find something you will love. Did it come with oils?"

"Yes, but just a couple of bottles. I didn't like the menthol smelling one. I used the lavender though."

"That was probably eucalyptus," Denise said. "It's very strong. Sounds like you would like something more soothing. Feel free to open the test bottles and try anything you see. You might like a citrus scent like these over here." Denise led her to a tester to try. "Do you plan to try other things with the oils? You know there are a lot of products you can make and different uses for essential oils, aside from just scenting the air."

"Oh, I don't know," Amanda said cautiously. "What do you recommend?"

"Well, I'm sure you buy personal products that you could make instead and have them all contain the scent you prefer. You know the scents have healing powers. Some are good as topical treatments too."

"No, I didn't know that."

"Oh, yes. If you need help sleeping or have headaches. There are oils that will help."

"No, no problems really. I just like to have it smelling nice."

"Well, then we just need to find something that pleases you. You know we can mix the oils and make something just right for you."

Denise opened lots of different testers for Amanda to try to isolate three she liked most. Taking the three testers to the counter, she showed Amanda how to mix them together until they got the blend she preferred.

"Are these oils different?" Amanda point to the bottles on the lower shelves that matched the brand label on the Chief's cypress oil.

"Oh, no," Denise said, shaking her head. "They are just a different company. All the oils here are 100% pure therapeutic grade."

"I'll take these three," Amanda said, pointing at the testers on the counter. "But since the mixture takes twice as much lavender, I think I'll need the larger bottle." Amanda pointed at the oils on the lower shelf that offered a large size. "Will this brand smell the same as these testers?"

"Certainly," Denise said as Amanda added the bottle to the counter and presented her coupon. "Oh, do you go to Louise's Beauty Shop? I left those there and hoped someone would use them."

"Yes, my mom…"

"See on the back there is a recipe. There are a lot of things you use your oils for so they can be a part of your every day life. A lot of people think they can't make something like this, but even if you just buy unscented products, you can always add your special scent to them."

"These little plants," Amanda said fondling the velvety leaf of a sage plant that was sitting beside the credit card machine, "They are so cute."

"Aren't they? They smell lovely, too," Denise said as Amanda leaned forward to try to breathe in the scent despite all the many competing aromas in the store. "That's a sage plant. They come from the Stotlar Tree Farm north of town. There are several sitting around the store. Sage is made into an essential oil too."

"Really?"

"Yes, but most people want the little plants so they have fresh sage for cooking, I think. He's planning to try drying some herbs and maybe I'll have them available in the store if you're interested."

"Well, thank you," Amanda said as Denise handed her a receipt. "I've got to get back to work."

"Thank you and come back when you need more." Denise waved as Amanda reached for the door, "or when you want to try a new scent."

"I will," Amanda assured her as she pulled the chiming door shut behind her and darted across the street to the Caraway Café to pick up her sandwich order. As she came out of the café to walk back to work with her lunch in a brown bag, she saw Bryan Stotlar walking into Ivy's Oils & Organics with a box in his hands. She had missed him again by just minutes.

Maybe that was for the best.

Chapter Fourteen

"Hey, Denise," Bryan said as the entrance bells jingled over his head. "I just brought these in to drop off. The lady that you spoke to earlier this week is stopping in to pick them up."

"Oh, okay." Denise peered into the box. "While you're here, let me give you what you've made." She handed him an envelope where she saved the money received on his plants, less her commission. "I'm sorry I had to call. What should I tell folks if they ask again?"

"That was fine. You can give them my number. I don't mind. I don't open until March, but I'm happy to bring in something if someone needs it."

"That's good. I'll do that. Have you started on the herbs yet?"

"I've started drying them, yes. I don't have any ready yet though. I did check with City Hall and there shouldn't be any conflict with your license if you'd like to put some in the store."

"Oh, that's great," Denise said over her ringing phone. "I think they'd be a good addition."

"I'll let you know." Bryan placed the extra plants he'd brought around the store as she answered her phone. He felt the soil in each pot to ensure they were not too dry as he waited a moment to see if Denise's call was going to be short.

He didn't mean to eavesdrop but he couldn't help but hear her conversation.

"Not now, Harvey... Yes, tonight... I'll call you."

As Denise hung up the phone, Bryan waved goodbye and opened the door. "Call if you need anything," he said after the door jingled.

"I will. Thanks," Denise yelled as he walked out into the cold. The wind was blowing fiercely, and he tucked the flaps of his coat closed over his chest. He needed to check the weather and see if snow was coming.

"Mandy, I'll be up on the second floor if you need me," Cora hollered out her office door as she gathered her papers and files together for her meeting. She was rushed as usual and brushed cracker crumbs from her skirt as she stood. There had been no time for lunch and she had eaten peanut butter crackers she found in her desk drawer to hold her over.

"Okay," Amanda said as Cora entered her outer office.

"Glad to see someone got lunch," Cora said. "I'm going to be starving before this is over. Maybe I should take some water."

"There are some cold bottles in the refrigerator in the break room."

"I'll grab one on my way up. If I'm not out of there by closing time, you have a good weekend now." Cora bustled around the corner and down the back hallway to the break room.

Once Amanda was alone in the office, she finished her sandwich and looked out in the lobby to see if it was busy. She was anxious to test the products she purchased, but she liked to let them dry for at least an hour. Cora's planning commission meeting would last much of the afternoon and she just couldn't wait until she got home that evening.

She used her lunch plate to protect her desk and got a piece of white paper out of the copy machine. After drawing three circles on the paper labeled with the names of the oil, she placed a drop in each circle and left the paper to dry. She glanced at the clock and made a mental note to check them in an hour. She wanted to be certain to give them adequate time before judging them.

She wasn't certain what Chief Harris or Cora would do with the information and that made her hesitant to tell them. At first, she told Cora just to dissuade her from buying more if they were inferior, but Cora had clearly wanted to do more than just alter her buying habits. She had wanted to right a wrong and now had gotten Chief Harris involved.

Pushing her hands through her hair, she massaged the tension away in her temples. She didn't want to be responsible for someone getting into trouble with the law. It was always possible that Denise didn't know, but she used them all the time. She should have noticed the difference.

At the end of the day, Cora had not returned yet and Amanda prepared to close up the office. Cora had a key to let herself back in but the girls in the lobby were closing the front doors and busy talking about their weekend plans. Walking to the copy machine, she picked up her test paper carefully and looked at the results. She was not surprised to find that the large bottle of lavender that held a label like the one on the Chief's cypress had tested pure, while the others with the purple labels had not. She placed her hand across her stomach as she felt her muscles clinch with anxiety.

The mayor would have to be told Monday.

Chapter Fifteen

Amanda drove home deep in thought. She didn't know what to do with this new knowledge. She didn't have to share it with anyone. No one knew that she'd gone shopping or snooping at Ivy's today. She wondered what impact all of this could have on Bryan if he was doing business with her.

She would usually discuss this type of thing with Cora. She'd long ago given up talking to her mother. Louise couldn't stop herself from sharing everything she knew even if it hurt the ones she loved. She never understood how devastating her gossip had been to Amanda when she ruined her senior year in high school by sharing her thoughts with the whole beauty shop and destroying her senior prom.

At this point in her life, her relationship with her mother was pleasant, although distant, because she didn't share anything personal at all. Even though she saw now that her life hadn't been wrecked forever by high school gossip, the hurt was deep and her memory still very clear. The betrayal would always cloud their inter-personal connection for her.

"Hi, honey," her mom called out from the kitchen when Amanda came in the front door and took off her coat. "Dinner will be at least a half hour or so. I'm just getting started and your dad's not home yet."

"Okay, mom," Amanda called out as she walked up the stairs. She changed into her comfortable yoga pants and sweatshirt first before rolling out her yoga mat on her bedroom floor. She needed the peace and quiet to decide if holding back her information was really the best thing to do. She didn't know Bryan well enough to be certain he wasn't personally involved with Denise. Sharing something with Bryan with the innocent intention of protecting him could mean that she would betray Cora and the Chief if Bryan shared it with Denise.

She felt some uncertainty about talking to Bryan at all. He hadn't called or stopped in to see her and she'd made a terrible impression on their date. She did want to rectify that some way. Even if he wasn't interested in seeing her again, she hated to leave things the way they were between them.

In the middle of her cool down pose, she decided she would drive out to his place in the morning. If he was there, she'd give him a chance to actually talk this time and then she could tell whether he was involved with Denise. She could always ask about his plants in Ivy's Oils & Organics and see if he would tell her about his plans for the spring. His reaction to her visit would tell her a lot about where their relationship stood, and she hoped they could at least be friends.

Walking down the stairs, the spicy aroma of chili powder snaked around her and she heard her father talking on the phone in the living room. The kitchen was warm and bright, but her mother's forehead was beaded with perspiration as she lined up bowls down the kitchen island. Each bowl held a different garnish, and the counter was sprinkled with remnants of all the chopping her mother had done.

"What are you cooking?" Amanda regretted her accusatory tone, but this was not normal dinner presentation in the Morgan household. Her parents were very traditional in most respects and dinner usually consisted of a meat dish and a couple of sides arranged on the table.

"Linda gave me a new recipe and I'm trying it out," Louise said as her father, Hymie, walked into the kitchen. "It's chicken tacos! It's a new year and I'm going to try new things. We always eat the same stuff all the time. Linda said this was really good and her family loved it."

"Hmm," Hymie grunted as he peered over the skillet and sniffed. "Smells spicy."

"You love spicy," Louise countered and handed him three plates to take to the table. "Now you just put a tortilla on your plate and add the chicken first. Then go down the counter and spoon the other stuff on top."

"And how do I eat this pile of food once I dump everything on top?"

"Well, I don't know," Louise said flustered with the image it created. "We'll figure that out once we do it."

"You can roll it up, Dad," Amanda said trying to help, "or you can just cut the tortilla with a knife and pretend it's a casserole."

"Okay, let's give it a try." Hymie rubbed his hands together in anticipation.

Amanda took a plate and started so she could demonstrate. Before she had her meat arranged on the tortilla, her father was back to analyzing.

"What's this?" Hymie pointed to the last two bowls on the counter.

"That's avocado, and that's a cilantro mix that you put on top." Louise pointed with a wooden spoon. "That's sour cream there, if you'd rather have that but I think you'll like the cilantro sauce. Here," she said dipping the spoon into the bowl and thrusting it towards Hymie's face. "Taste it."

Amanda topped the meat in her tortilla with corn and black beans but stood waiting for her parents to accept the challenge and move down the line. Once her father gave into the change, he joined her in line with his plate and slowly sampled each bowl until they were all seated at the table.

"See, you like it, don't you?" Louise nodded with a smug grin. "I knew you would when Linda told me about it. You like all these things. You just balk at the idea of mixing it all up. If I'd put all this in a dish and baked it together, you wouldn't have thought a thing about it."

"You're probably right," Hymie nodded in defeat. "It's sure messy, but it tastes good."

"I told you," Louise goaded.

"But maybe next time you could try that baking it all together thing." Hymie smiled at Amanda and winked as her mother sputtered.

"What are you doing tomorrow, Mandy? I'm thinking about going over to Paxton around noon so I can get a few things at that big food mart over there. I just have one morning appointment."

"Are we trying a new recipe tomorrow night too?" Hymie winced a little. Louise ignored his comment and looked at Amanda.

"I've got some errands to run in the morning and I don't know if I'll be back when you're ready to leave." Amanda didn't really want to go, but she knew her mother would like the company. She didn't really know what tomorrow would hold yet.

"Errands? Well, what do you need to do? We can go do those on our way," Louise said with a dismissive wave of her hand.

"No, that's okay. I plan to do some things in the morning. I don't know when I'll be back." Amanda tensed anticipating further interrogation.

"Okay," Louise sighed and let her shoulders slump. "I'll text you before I go and you can let me know then."

"Okay." Amanda pushed back her chair to take her plate to the sink.

"Are you going anywhere tonight?"

"No." Amanda clenched her teeth wishing these inquisitions didn't bother her so much. "Do you want me to do the dishes?"

"No, honey. I'm just going to load the dishwasher and put up the leftovers. I think there's enough for you to have for lunch tomorrow." Louise patted Hymie's hand and smiled. Hymie just nodded as he chewed, quietly appreciating that his pushy wife always kept him fed.

"All right, then." Amanda slipped her plate into the stand on the bottom of the dishwasher rack. "I'll be upstairs."

"I think we're going to watch a movie later, if you want to join us," Louise said.

Amanda headed up the steps without responding. She knew her mother didn't really expect her to come back. She had a TV and a computer in her bedroom and rarely joined them in the evenings.

Chapter Sixteen

As Conrad drove to town Saturday morning, he heard a tag called over the police radio and although he wasn't intentionally listening, the numbers jumped out at him, Papa-Oscar-Yankee-5718. The request for a tag search was coming from a young officer named Darren Hudson and Conrad grabbed his radio. "Possible Code Five. What's your location?"

"Fennel Street, 400 block"

"Stand by." Conrad inched the gas pedal down just a little more. He was already headed to Fennel Street looking for breakfast. As he approached, he saw Officer Hudson's car blocking the white truck in a parking place in front of the Fennel Street Bakery but there was no driver inside. Pulling up to face his squad car to Officer

Hudson's car, he answered his ringing phone as he got out of the car.

"Hey, Georgie."

"Roy is in route. He just heard the call in the office."

"Okay, thanks." Conrad walked over to the truck to inspect the license plate and motioned for Officer Hudson to follow. He knew Georgia would have explained the situation to him already, but he needed to see for himself. He ran his fingers over the plates and felt the indentations vary. He knew then that he had been right.

"Have you seen him?" Conrad looked around the streets to see if he was walking in the area.

"No, Chief. I just saw the truck."

"I bet I know where he is. Stay with the vehicle," Conrad said and headed over to Ivy's Oils & Organics. Conrad saw him through the window before he even opened the door.

"Excuse me," Conrad said once the overhead doorbell jingle announced him. Denise was behind the counter and Shawn Ellis was facing her. They both looked at the door when they heard the chime.

"Chief Harris," Denise said cheerily. "How nice to see you again."

Conrad gave Denise a smiling nod and looked directly at Shawn Ellis who was peering uncomfortably at him. "Mr. Ellis, could you please step outside with me a moment?"

Conrad always tried to use the kind approach in the beginning, especially when innocent bystanders were involved, but he didn't have much patience for it.

"Uh, in a minute. I need to finish my business here first." Shawn had turned away so spoke over his shoulder to Conrad to avoid eye contact and turned back to Denise.

Conrad waved his hand at Denise Ivy to motion her away from the counter as she gave him a frightened stare. "Mr. Ellis, step outside." Conrad hadn't advanced from the doorway yet because Ellis still had his back to him and he wasn't certain he didn't have a weapon. He could have something in his waistband or under his coat.

"Outside—Now," Roy barked as he pushed past the Chief and placed his hands on Ellis' shoulders to turn him around. Once Roy spun him around, he checked his coat and waist for weapons and Conrad followed Roy out the door as he pushed him to the sidewalk.

"Sorry to interrupt." Conrad nodded a goodbye to Denise as he closed the door to her store and left her standing in shock.

Roy put cuffs on Ellis and pushed him in the back of his squad car without offering any explanation. Conrad thought it odd that Ellis didn't even ask why he was being thrown in the back of a police squad car. Perhaps he knew there were several reasons he belonged there.

"I didn't see you pull up," Conrad said once Roy slammed the car door.

"Just got here, Chief. Hudson told me where you were."

"Let's take him back and let him sit awhile," Conrad said. "Maybe he'll start to wonder why we picked him up." Roy nodded and opened his car door. "Maybe there's more to him than we know."

§

Amanda waited until she heard her mother's car pull out of the garage before she ventured downstairs for breakfast. She didn't want to face questions, and that was all her mother seemed to offer. Her father left really early on Saturdays as he always had a full schedule of appointments as the town's veterinarian. She had resented it as a child but admired it in him now.

She had thought all night about her approach today and decided she would cautiously talk with Bryan first. She would have to see how he responded before she shared anything related to Ivy's Oils. She knew it would be awkward showing up at his house, especially when the farm wasn't open yet, but she couldn't get the closure she needed if she didn't. This visit wasn't just to share a warning. It was also an opportunity she needed to correct all the missteps she'd taken with him.

A little after 9:00 she decided it was safe to go. She was going to stop at the Fennel Street Bakery and buy some lemon puffs to take with her. She remembered him saying when they had dinner on New Year's Eve that those had been a favorite of his and she thought they would make an appropriate offering to ease her unexpected visit.

When she turned onto Fennel Street, she saw the lights of the police cars blocking traffic in front of Ivy's Oils & Organics as well as the bakery. She was two blocks away but she could tell there were three separate cars there and two had lights on. She saw uniformed men walking out of Ivy's store with someone but the other cars parked against the curb were blocking her view. She couldn't tell who it was, but it looked like someone was getting arrested.

She turned at the intersection and headed north to the Stotlar Tree Farm. She put all of her coy plans aside and just hoped it wasn't too late to save Bryan. He needed to know that Ivy's was not a good place to look for business connections or any other kind of connection. She wasn't even worried about the mayor or the police chief now.

§

Cora was glued to the window in the Caraway Café across the street with a cinnamon roll growing soggy in her left hand while she warmed her right hand around her cup of tea. She was only mildly entertained by the initial stop, but seeing Conrad pull up and get involved had paused her breakfast. He didn't involve himself in commonplace skirmishes unless they had some hidden significance. When he entered Ivy's Oils & Organics, she couldn't take another bite.

She remembered their lunch when Conrad had watched Denise's shop the whole time because he was concerned with someone who went in there. She wondered if that man had returned. Maybe she needed to go check on poor Denise.

Chapter Seventeen

Amanda's mind was overtaken with images of Bryan being handcuffed. What if he had been there? She hadn't seen who they arrested. Denise was new to town. No one knew her. Maybe she was a criminal. Even worse, maybe the Chief had found out something more than her retail items being counterfeit and this had all spun out of control. She was so caught up in all the possibilities that she drove right by Bryan's farm and had to turn around on a country lane.

Driving back more slowly, she looked at the house but didn't see his truck. The alarm gripped her again. What if he was up at Ivy's? What if it was him, they put in that squad car?

No, why would anyone arrest Bryan? That couldn't have happened. But what was going on? If anyone knew, it was probably her mother. She knew everything that went on in Spicetown.

Amanda pulled off the road into a gravel area near the greenhouse and then she saw Bryan's truck pulled around on the side. She was just going to relay her information and apologize at the same time. All the other pretend conversations she had fabricated in her mind last night were pushed aside. Now, where was he?

He didn't answer the door when she rang the bell so she walked around the greenhouse to see if he was around the back. Just as she walked around the corner of the building, the greenhouse door opened and she jumped.

"Oh. You scared me."

"Sorry. I heard a car, but I had my hands in dirt so I couldn't get to the door. Come in. It's warmer in here."

"I'm sorry I'm just showing up like this unannounced... uninvited. I don't mean to intrude. I just came from town and..."

"You're always welcome. Don't be silly." Bryan dried off his hands. "Here. Have a seat. I'm just repotting some plants I propagated. I'm glad you came."

"Well, I was curious. I did want to see your plants. I saw the little ones in Ivy's Oils & Organics. They're adorable."

"Thank you. They seem to sell pretty well in her store."

"That's the other reason I'm here," Amanda said hesitating. She was calmer now and needed to choose her words carefully. "Have you talked to her lately?"

"I was up there yesterday. A lady needed six more plants and so I dropped them off there for her to pick up. We didn't really talk. She knew I was bringing them. Why?"

"Well, I just drove by there. I mean I tried to drive by there but Fennel Street was blocked with police cars. It looked to me like someone got arrested in her store, but I couldn't see who they put in the car."

"Wow, some excitement in Spicetown," Bryan said smiling. He seemed unconcerned about Denise or the arrest. Amanda took that to mean he couldn't care much about her, so she kept going.

"I didn't know whether you two were close or not. I had heard you were thinking of doing business with her and that's another reason…"

"No, nothing much. I just put a few plants in there for the winter. I had asked her if she wanted some dried herbs or preserves when they're ready. They might sell better in town than out here, but I don't know her well."

"That's good. I wouldn't want you to get into business with someone that got arrested."

"*She* got arrested?"

"No, uh, I don't know. Someone in her store did but I couldn't see who they brought out. They put someone in a squad car out front but I couldn't drive by."

"You'll have to ask your mom." Bryan smirked jokingly. Amanda had told him all about her mother's gossip mill when they had been at dinner.

"Yeah, I'm sure she'll hear about it. I'll let you know when I hear." Amanda laughed and relaxed. He was really very easy to talk to when she wasn't so focused on making a good impression.

"Can I have a tour? I'd love to see what you have in here."

"Sure." Bryan held out his arm to steer her towards a long white table in the back of the greenhouse. "I was just working on these little plants. I propagate from this larger plant to make those little sage plants I put in Denise's store."

"Those are so cute. I saw them when I was in there. How do you propagate?"

"I just cut the mother plant here," he said pointing to a place on the large sage plant, "and put the cutting in water a couple of weeks for it to root." He held up a glass that held some small plants with white roots floating in water.

"That's really cool." Amanda held them up higher. "I can help you. I do know how to pot a plant. I didn't realize you could make a bunch of plants out of one though."

"Not everything works that way, but most plants will root easily." Bryan brushed dirt from the table and lined up small pots beside the bag of soil on the table.

"You have to be gentle with the roots. They get tangled together sometimes and here… Let me show you." Bryan put some soil in a tiny pot and turned it sideways to add soil to just one side as he carefully placed the plant in with roots splayed out neatly before adding more soil.

"The leaves will hold dirt, so you have to try and keep the soil off the plant leaves." He handed her a completed pot to demonstrate and used a tiny scoop to add soil until it leveled off.

"Adorable," Amanda said as she brushed soil from the outside of the pot onto the table. "You know, these would really look nice with a ribbon tied around them. You could use different colors or prints and just tie a bow."

"You're probably right. I'll add that to my orders."

"When it gets close to a holiday, you could make the ribbon match or get those little plastic spikes to put in the soil that say 'Happy Saint Pat's Day' or whatever the holiday is. They'd be easy to change out once the holiday is over."

Bryan smiled at Amanda's suggestions and nodded to her, pleased she had taken an interest. She was a different person today than she had been on their date. She had been preoccupied with everything going on around her at the restaurant and at the county fireworks that night. Her eyes had darted everywhere but into his. Today was different, and he was enjoying this time with her.

"Have you ever thought about painting the pots? They're just clay and I'm sure they'd take paint well."

"Oh, I don't have any artistic ability." Bryan shook his head. "You wouldn't want to see me paint anything except maybe the barn."

"It would be just like decorating Easter eggs. I love to do that."

"When I was a kid, my Easter eggs were all just a solid color," Bryan chuckled.

"Oh, it'll be fun," Amanda teased him with a nudge of her elbow. "I'll help you."

Bryan took her around the greenhouse and explained what each plant was and what his plans were. There were small trees starting out inside to keep them warm and small bushes he hoped would be used in landscaping projects.

They went inside his house for some hot chocolate and he showed her his first attempts at drying herbs. There were three different ways to do it and he was experimenting with each to see what produced the best quality.

She asked a million questions and offered a few suggestions that set Bryan's mind whirling. It was nice to have someone he could share things with regarding the expansion and her interest prompted him to roll out his entire plan across the kitchen table. She studied everything and had several ideas about additional items he could explore as well as ways to cut costs. Her analytical mind was a godsend to him and he feverishly took notes on her ideas.

"I wish I had a project like this," Amanda said wistfully. She loved her job but her personal life was rather empty since returning to Spicetown. "Starting something new like this must be so much fun."

"Well, I can't say I'm having fun yet exactly. I do spend a lot of time thinking, planning and surfing the internet. It's been a little stressful to be honest."

"It's your business. I understand that," Amanda said nodding. "I think it's exciting though, and I'd love to help."

Amanda's eagerness was a bit overwhelming. Bryan had never expected anyone to find his plants interesting. "Of course, I'd love to have help," he answered after a brief pause.

"I don't mean to be pushy." Amanda recoiled from the bewildered look on Bryan's face. "I'm sorry. I just come in here and try take over. I am pushy sometimes. I just love what you're doing and if you need any help at all, even just moving dirt, I'd happy to help."

Bryan chuckled at the image he had of Amanda shoveling. With all her energy, he might just get everything done by spring. It warmed his heart to think she wanted to be around and was interested.

"No, you're not pushy at all. I'd love to have the help and even more to have the company. I'm out here puttering around alone all the time and it helps to have someone to talk to about things."

Amanda looked eager to start and had a faraway look in her eyes. "Let's finish your little plants and then if you'll let me, I'd like to take some empty pots home with me. I want to experiment a little with them."

"Sure, I've got plenty of them. You can take some with you, but we don't have to finish the plants today."

"No, I want to." Amanda sat her cup in his sink. "It won't take long and we should finish up. Let's go."

Bryan was glad she didn't want to leave and followed her out the back door with the biggest grin across his face.

§

"Hello, dear," Cora said to Denise as she pushed the jingling door shut. "How are you today?"

"Just fine, Mayor. How can I help you?"

"Well, I'm here to see if I can get some help. I bought those oils and the machine earlier, but my friend is having some problems with it. I hoped you could help."

"Of course." Denise nervously pushed her hair behind her ears. "What kind of problems? Is the machine not working for her?"

"Yes, it's running, but she says the oil scents aren't lasting. She wants something stronger. I told her I'd ask you about that. Is there something different she can try?"

"Sure. We can try a different brand and see if that makes a difference for her. Let me see what I can find for you." Denise darted around the counter and began checking the labels of various bottles to pull. Cora leaned her elbow on the counter and watched her. As she expected, Denise was pulling only those bottles that had the brand label that matched Conrad's Cypress oil. Denise knew the good from the bad.

"It looked like you had a bit of trouble this morning." Cora tried to sound casual. "Did you have a shoplifter in here?"

"Oh, no. I don't know what that was about. There was a gentleman in here shopping and the police just came in and picked him up. I don't know anything about it."

"They arrested him?"

"It appeared so," Denise shrugged with an innocent smile.

"Not anyone you knew or had seen before?"

"Oh no. I've never seen him before," Denise said avoiding Cora's eyes. "It happened so fast that he didn't even get a chance to buy anything." Denise smiled and walked back to the counter carrying three small boxes.

"No, charge." Denise held up her hand to stop Cora from diving into her purse. "Please take these to your friend and have her try them. I think these are more concentrated and she should be pleased, but if she's not, please let me know."

Cora smiled through gritted teeth and tossed the little boxes in her oversized handbag. "I will do that. Thank you and you have a good day."

Sheri Richey

Chapter Eighteen

"Chief, how long do you want to wait to talk to Ellis? Roy is off in an hour and he wants to be there," Officer Hudson said peering around the corner of Conrad's office door.

"Has he said anything yet? Asked any questions?"

"Not a word. He's just sitting in holding. Hasn't even asked for a lawyer."

"Roy doesn't need to be there," Conrad said. He'd prefer Roy not be there because he would probably be too aggressive for the situation. Roy was holding a grudge because he'd looked like a fool when he jumped on Georgia about those plates when it wasn't her fault. None of that had anything to do with Shawn Ellis. "Let's give it a couple of hours. He'll be hungry and we might be able to use that."

"Okay, Chief." Hudson walked back to dispatch.

Conrad planned to order a pizza and let Ellis smell it for a while before starting his questioning. If he behaved, he might even offer him a piece.

It was odd that he hadn't asked for representation though. A man like Ellis should have an attorney to contact, especially with all of his criminal history.

When his desk phone rang, he hoped it would be Wink so he could ask him to clock in a little early. He wanted him to be with him when he questioned Ellis. Hudson didn't have enough experience, and he worked well with Wink when they were paired.

"Chief Harris." Conrad read the number listed on the phone display just as he answered and had but a split second to prepare himself for Sheriff Bell.

"Connie, I hear you have your hands on Shawn Ellis."

"Evening, Sheriff. Yes, I do indeed. You have an interest in Ellis?" Once an arrest was made, the word went out, and the county monitored their activity even if no charges had been filed. But in this case, they were holding Ellis on driving with no license and tampering with vehicle tags with intent to conceal. The felony charge wouldn't hold up once he provided a title to the truck, but it bought Conrad some time.

"I do," Bobby growled. "I want to talk to him. Hang onto him. We're on our way."

Conrad barely had a chance to utter consent before Bobby Bell disconnected the call. Apparently, his compliance wasn't questioned.

§

When Amanda arrived home, she could smell something spicy cooking again. She didn't know why her mother had decided to change everything up all of a sudden, but she didn't mind. She wasn't certain her father was all in yet though.

"Hi, mom," Amanda called from the door as she took off her coat. "I'm home."

"Good," Louise yelled back. "We eat in about ten minutes. I was getting worried."

"Okay. Be right there." Amanda dropped her purse at the foot of the stairs and went out the side door to the garage. She still had boxes out there from when she moved home from college and she thought there might be some craft supplies packed away. Although her roommate, Roxanne, did most of the assembly, Amanda found she enjoyed decorating the crafts once they were completed.

Rummaging in the boxes, she found twine, ribbon and a small paint kit that she hoped hadn't dried out yet. Tossing it all in a sack, she tucked it by her purse on the stairs and went in the kitchen to help her mother with dinner.

She had felt so energized hearing of Bryan's plans today. They had laughed and talked about everything. She told him about college. He told her about his family and how he grew up. She told him funny stories about her father's farm calls and her mother's beauty salon drama, while he told her about the pranks he used to play on his mother.

Every time she had looked into his eyes, she marveled at how they gleamed and it grew brighter when he smiled. The time had flown by and when the sun began to set, she knew she had to get home or her mother would be texting her. She had checked her phone a couple of times afraid that she'd silenced the ringer. She hadn't heard anything from her mom all day and that was unusual, especially when she didn't know where Amanda was.

As they sat down to dinner and Louise explained to Hymie what an enchilada contained to reassure him he would like it, Amanda tried to redirect the conversation.

"Do we have any glue around the house?" Both of her parents looked at her in puzzlement. "Not just white glue, but something really strong?"

"Why, honey? Did you break something?" Her mother turned towards her as her father began to test the new meal.

"No, I'm just in a creative mood. I'd like to do some crafting again and my glue is dried up." *I wish Mom would just answer the question instead of demanding an explanation first.*

"There's some nail glue in the kitchen drawer by the phone," her mother offered and raised an eyebrow to Hymie.

"I don't know of any. Maybe something in the garage on the shelf but it might be dried up too."

Hymie shrugged and took another bite. "This isn't too bad."

"What a back-handed compliment," Louise said giggling. "I knew you'd like it. You should learn to trust me."

Hymie just nodded and continued to eat.

"So, what are you going to make?" Louise asked with raised eyebrows.

"I am going to decorate some flower pots. I don't know exactly what I'm going to do yet but I'm thinking about it. I'm going to search online after we eat and see if I get some ideas."

"Are these for Bryan?" Louise stretched out his name in a sing-song voice as she said it and turned to smile at Hymie.

Amanda felt her jaws clinch. Her mother obviously guessed she had been there today. Probably someone saw her car there on their way to the beauty shop and had to report it. That's why she hadn't texted her.

"Yes, he has these cute little potted herbs that he sells and I think they would look nice if they were decorated a little. I told him I'd think about it and see what I could do."

Hymie kept his eyes on his plate and concentrated on the meal.

"I'm sure you can pretty them up, dear. It's nice of you to help him."

Suddenly she remembered what made her go to Bryan's this morning. "Mom, did you hear anything about somebody being arrested on Fennel Street this morning? The road was blocked when

I tried to drive down and it looked like they were arresting somebody."

"Yes, I heard it was some customer in Ivy's Oils. No one from Spicetown as far as I know, just a visitor. I don't know anything more than that. Did you hear anything, Hymie?"

"No," Hymie said before wiping his mouth with a napkin. "Animals don't talk."

"Oh, honey," Louise said waving her hand dismissively at him. "You talk to people, too."

"Do you want help with dishes tonight?" Amanda asked as she got up from the table.

"No, you go Google, or whatever it is you do," Louise said smiling. "I'll take care of it."

"Thanks, mom. Dinner was good."

"Thank you, dear," Louise said as Amanda headed for the stairs.

"You know it may be really serious with Amanda and Bryan. She spent the whole day out there today," Louise said after Amanda's footsteps could be heard on the stairs.

"That's nice." Hymie seemed unaffected by Louise's comment and pushed his chair back from the table.

"Maybe," Louise murmured as she stared out the darkened dining room window.

§

"Connie," Sheriff Bell boomed out as he walked across the dispatch room to vigorously shake Conrad's hand. "Good to see you."

The display was for the benefit of the staff. "And you, Sheriff."

"Do you have Ellis in a room? We'd like to talk to him."

"No, but I can have him pulled up here pretty quick." Conrad nodded at Officer Hudson. Darren swiftly left the room to bring Shawn Ellis from holding to an interview room.

"Do you want some coffee?"

"Yeah, that would be great. This here is Detective Young," Bobby said in introduction of his companion. Conrad stepped forward to shake, but soon realized Detective Young was not reciprocating and nodded his greeting instead.

"We can go in my office if you like," Conrad offered as a way to fill the time needed to seat the suspect in a room. He hoped Bobby would tell him what he was planning to question Shawn Ellis about.

Bobby just nodded and then silently instructed Detective Young to stay in dispatch as he followed Conrad down the hall.

"How do take your coffee?" Conrad asked as Bobby Bell took off his coat and sat in a chair.

"Just black is fine. What made you snag Ellis today? What have you got him on?"

- 153 -

"Well," Conrad sighed as he sat down at his desk. "Not much. He's been lurking around town here and stands out a little. We tried to run his plates and found he'd altered them. After we pulled him, we found his license is suspended. I think there's more to him, but that's all I'm holding him for."

"You always had good instincts," Bobby nodded. "He's rotten, but I think he's my New Year's Eve thief. If he's not, I think he knows who is."

Conrad remembered then that Wink had shared a story on New Year's Eve about a white truck in the alley off Clove Street. That was near the same area that they picked him up in today.

"Did you ever find the fireworks?"

"No, but we've tracked them through a few hands. I think they were sold and have left the state by now. I'd like to nail it down though."

"He's in the room, Chief," Hudson said from the doorway.

"Do you want us to go in first? We haven't talked to him at all about the plates yet." Conrad thought they might want to watch for a few minutes just to assess the situation. That's what he would do. He knew his charges weren't serious but it would test the waters and give Bobby a minute to decide his approach.

"No," Bobby said standing to stretch out his shoulders. "I'd like to go on in. I think he'll know who I am and realize pretty quick that this isn't about his vehicle."

Conrad wasn't surprised by the boldness. Bobby would puff out his chest and imagine he was taller as he swaggered through the door. He only had one persona to play. A good interviewer went in softly and molded the tactic to the responses. Not Bobby. He tried to strong-arm everything and everyone.

"You can watch if you like." Bobby smiled as he walked to the door for Officer Hudson to lead him.

Conrad had seen the Bobby Bell show before and didn't like reruns. Instead he warmed up his coffee and sat down to check his email.

Sheri Richey

Chapter Nineteen

Amanda spent all day Sunday decorating little pots. She ran to Paxton for more supplies and even bought a few new pots when she found small square ones in the craft store. They were a nice change and much easier to decorate. She found holiday embellishments for the approaching Valentine's Day and could just envision the little plant added to a holiday gift of soaps and oils.

What Bryan really needed she decided was a business logo. She could draw fairly well and sat down to look through images on the computer of what other landscapers used. She became so engrossed with clicking and reading the websites of nurseries that hours passed before she knew it.

After dinner she started on a logo and expanded it to a website design. Bryan needed all of these things and he needed to do it in a couple of months. Spring was just around the corner.

When she went downstairs for a drink, her mother walked into the kitchen just as she was pulling out a gingerbread cookie from the pantry.

"Mandy, do you know anyone named Shawn Ellis? He's a little older than you, but…"

"No. That doesn't ring any bells with me. I've never heard of him. Why?"

"Well, he was the guy arrested yesterday in Ivy's Oils. It was in today's paper. I thought maybe you knew him."

"He must not be from here," Amanda suggested. There was only one high school in town and if her mother didn't know him, he couldn't live in town.

"I guess he wandered through the wrong town." Louise smiled and opened the refrigerator door.

"I meant to ask you, are you and Bryan dating now?"

Amanda was startled by the question initially, but then knew her mother must have heard she'd been at Bryan's house Saturday.

"No, mom. We're not dating. I'm just helping him out. He's expanding his business this spring and I just want to help."

"It's okay if you are," Louise said holding up her hand in a trepid wave. "He seems like a nice guy."

"He is." Amanda relaxed seeing her mother was prepared to back down.

"Bring your little pots down when you're done. I'd like to see them."

"Okay. I plan to run them out there tomorrow after work. I think they look really cute." Amanda smiled and couldn't help complimenting herself a little. She was anxious for Bryan to see them.

§

When Conrad arrived for work Monday morning, Roy was pacing around dispatch waiting for him.

"Chief!"

Conrad saw Officer Roy Asher bolt down the hallway towards him when he came in the side door. Shawn Ellis was still in the holding cell but would be arraigned that day for the vehicle charges. He knew Roy wanted to be updated on their interrogation.

"Morning, Roy."

"Chief, did you talk to Ellis? What did he say? I heard the sheriff wanted him, too. What do they have on him?"

"Settle down, Roy. I talked to him, but he didn't talk back." Conrad slowly removed his coat and sat down to turn on his computer.

"Did he ask for an attorney?"

"No, he just didn't talk to us at all. He knows we don't have anything on him—At least nothing he's afraid of and he's not a novice."

"Does the county have something on him?"

"I don't know. The sheriff talked to him but I haven't heard any more on it. I wasn't here when they left, so I don't know if Ellis talked to him or not."

"The guy's rotten, Chief."

"Maybe so," Conrad said nodding, "but I'm sure he'll walk with a fine at his hearing today. We just need to keep an eye on him if he comes back to Spicetown."

"Sure thing, Chief." Roy dropped his head as he left Conrad's office.

§

"Good morning, Amanda," Cora Mae said as she walked through the door to her office. "Did you have a good weekend?"

"I did and I have all your data ready for the budget meeting. It's printing out now, but I also emailed it to you. Do you think you have everything you need?"

"Not entirely and I want to get your perspective on something. Have a seat." Cora sat down at her desk and turned on her computer. As it beeped to boot up, she put up her purse and began emptying her satchel.

"I'd like to use your marketing degree, Mandy," Cora said smiling. "I have something I'd like to get done and I'm pretty sure the City Council is not going to help me."

"Okay." Amanda nodded although she felt her heart rate increase at the challenge. She didn't want to let Cora down, but she'd didn't feel like she'd ever really used that marketing degree she earned.

"Well, you know I've always said I'd like to put a statue of John Spicer in town. I'm just wondering if maybe it couldn't be funded a different way. If I found the money, the Council's objections wouldn't matter."

"You mean like with a grant?" Amanda said wrinkling her forehead.

"Now, see. I didn't even think of that. You're helping already. Can we get grant money for something like that?"

"Maybe." Amanda stared up into the corner of the room searching her memory. "It's historical. I mean you're trying to mark history with it so there might be grant money for that."

"That's a grand idea," Cora said shaking her fist. "Will you check on that for me?"

"Sure," Amanda said as she rose from her chair. "Do you know anything about the Spicer family? I mean are there ancestors to him around here?"

"That's a good question." Cora stared off in deep thought. "I don't really know, but we need to find out."

"I was just thinking that the family might be wealthy and want to pay for the statue themselves."

"How do we track that down?"

"Let me see what I can find out," Amanda said, tingling from the excitement of a new task.

"Even if they aren't, we'd definitely want to invite them to the ceremony," Cora said chuckling.

"I already feel closer to my goal with your suggestions."

"Oh, I also wanted to tell you that I tested all those oils Friday." Amanda turned around at the door.

"Yes, dear. I almost forgot all about that." Cora jumped in her chair and pulled out the desk drawer where she had stashed her purse.

"It turns out that just the one Chief Harris gave me is testing pure. It's sitting on my desk if he should happen to come by and I don't see him."

"Okay. I'll be sure and tell him. Here are three more," Cora said pulling them from her purse and handing them over to Amanda. "I think these are probably okay, but I'd like you to test them, too."

"Did they come from Ivy's?"

"They did," Cora said smugly.

"Did you tell her that the other ones were fake?"

"No, not exactly." Cora smiled coyly. "I told her that my friend was looking for something stronger, something that would last longer. She gave these to me free."

"Really?"

"Oh yes. That girl definitely knows the good from the bad."

Amanda smiled at Cora's cynically arched eyebrow as she pulled the door shut quietly and Cora picked up her desk phone.

§

"Good morning, Connie," Cora said when Conrad answered his cell phone. "I know you're busy but I wanted to let you know that Amanda's tests on those oils showed they were all phony except for yours."

When Conrad didn't immediately respond, Cora continued to the covert topic that caused her call. She had read the newspaper this morning.

"I saw you Saturday in front of Ivy's. I was across the street in the café. Does this Ellis guy have anything to do with Denise?"

"Ellis isn't talking," Conrad said. "But he doesn't seem like the kind of guy that needs a weekly fix of essential oils."

"So, you arrested him for the plates and license. Is that all it was?" Cora wasn't buying it. There was more to it. There were two officers and a police chief out there handling the arrest. That didn't happen for a vehicle tag infraction.

"That's all we charged him with. He gets arraigned today."

"Hmm," Cora said loudly enough to make Conrad chuckle into the phone as she tried to fill in the words he wasn't saying. "I talked to Denise today."

"Did you go down there to tell her about the oils?" Conrad's words were laced with a warning.

"No. I just told her I was looking for something stronger. She gave me new bottles for free to try. Amanda is going to test those too, but the reason I'm telling you this…"

"Cora, you need to keep away from all this for a while. She's made the sale right now, and I'd feel better if you didn't go in there anymore until this is all sorted out."

"Well, I can't always make you feel better, Connie," Cora said sarcastically. He should know better than try to scold her by now. "Now listen. That girl told me that she had never seen Ellis before."

"You talked to her about the arrest?" Conrad sighed heavily with exasperation. "Cora…"

"Oh, hush. I just told her I'd seen she had some trouble earlier today. I did. *I* was telling the truth. I was in the Caraway when you arrested Ellis that morning."

"Ok," Conrad said in defeat. "And she said she'd never seen him before?"

"Yes, she lied to me. Then she said he had just gotten to the store when he got arrested. That's another lie. I saw him walk in there long before you guys showed up. You need to ask him if he knows Denise."

"Ok. Give me some time. Maybe I'll know more later today," Conrad said.

"Well, it's Monday, so perhaps we should have dinner at the Juniper Junction," Cora said with a smile on her face. She hoped Connie understood that she had uncovered where Saucy dined on Mondays.

"Perhaps we should," Conrad said with a smile in his voice. "You think we might see someone we know?"

"We might," Cora said satisfied that her message had been relayed. She just hoped Saucy wasn't tangled up with Shawn Ellis or in this strange story with Ivy's oils too much.

Sheri Richey

Chapter Twenty

"Denise," Harvey shouted. "Have you heard anything?"

"Yes, Harvey," Denise said slowly holding the phone away from her ear. Harvey could get agitated over the slightest things. "It was nothing, and he's out now."

"Nothing! They arrested him in *your* store! The whole town is talking about it. Everyone saw it."

"Ah, free publicity," Denise teased him in hopes he would relax. "They even got the name right."

"This is no laughing matter," Harvey huffed. Denise could visualize him pacing across his kitchen and looking out the windows to make certain no one was lurking about.

"I told you that guy was bad news. You can tell by looking at him that he's a criminal."

"Harvey, he just had expired tags or something. It's no big deal. Anyway, the reason I called is he said he'd come by tonight and move the boxes out. He's found somewhere else to store his stuff."

"Good—I don't want anything to do with him."

"I know. It'll be after 9:00 before he can get there because he has to get a truck."

"Okay," Harvey sighed. "Okay, I'll be here. But what about your oils out there?"

"He'll bring them to the store. Don't worry about it. It's all fine."

§

Amanda left the office as soon as the lobby closed and headed for Bryan's. She hadn't called him or told him she'd be by, but her back seat was jammed full of little decorated pots. Slowing down early to not miss the turn again, she spotted his truck and pulled in beside it.

Leaving the pots in the car, she scurried up to tap on the door. It was already nearly dark, and the temperature had dropped significantly. He opened the door just as she briskly rubbed her hands together.

"Hi," she said bunching her shoulders up around her neck. "I hope it's okay I stopped by."

"Sure."

"I decorated some pots I wanted to show you. They're out in the car."

"Here, you come inside. It's freezing. I'll get them out." Amanda didn't go inside but followed Bryan to the car.

"Wow! There's a lot of them," Bryan stepped back in awe when she opened the back door.

"I got carried away," Amanda said sheepishly, but quickly grabbed a box as they hurried inside the house.

Sitting the boxes on the kitchen table, he slowly took out each pot as she explained her intent with each design. Although he nodded occasionally, Bryan had a stunned look on his face.

"These are amazing, Amanda. You could sell just the pot. You don't even need a plant in them."

"Oh," Amanda waved a hand at him modestly and smiled.

"No, I mean it. These are incredible."

"Well, I'm glad you like them. I had a blast making them and I have a million ideas for more."

"What do I owe you?" Bryan asked. Amanda immediately held up her hand and shook her head. "This was a lot of work and a lot of time. I can't take these without paying you something."

"Absolutely not," Amanda said sternly. "I wanted to help. This wasn't work for me."

"It's like a fairy garden." Bryan swept his arms out over all the pots arranged out on his table.

"That's what we'll call them—fairy herbs." Amanda giggled and imagined all the little gnomes and fairies she could paint peeking around the edges of the planters.

"Speaking of naming things," Amanda said cautiously. "Are you changing your business name when you get all the new lines in and open for the spring?"

"It's just Stotlar's to me. It always has been. I guess it won't be Stotlar's Tree Farm anymore."

"I thought maybe you'd change it to Stotlar Nursery or Stotlar Gardens," Amanda shrugged her shoulders. "Either is fine, but I was just playing around with logos and things…"

"Logos?"

"Yes, you need a logo, business cards, website, a new sign…"

"Wait. I can't do all that. I'm just trying to get the plants lined up."

"I know, but these things need to be done, too. You need your new name and logo so you can put ads in the paper this spring. You need business cards and stationary to give people estimates on landscaping. There's a lot of that stuff that needs to be done quickly."

"I don't even know where to start." Bryan sat down at the table.

"Nonsense," Amanda said sitting down next to him. "It's easy stuff. I've already started some for you. Just tell me what you like." Amanda pulled her notebook out of her purse and opened the pad on the table.

"I just used the name Stotlar Nursery, but it can be changed easily. I just didn't know what you planned to call it." Flipping another page over, she pointed to the top drawing.

"See this one? It's an oval, but you can do the same in a circle shape or something more angular. Depends on what you like."

Bryan flipped through the pages as Amanda explained her approach on each design.

"Some I focused on landscaping specifically but others are just more nursery and plant purchase. I wasn't sure what emphasis you wanted."

"I don't really know either." Bryan ran his hands through his hair as he studied the samples. He continued flipping through the logos until he saw a design where she had used tiny Christmas trees to make the letter 'A' in his name.

"This one," Bryan said stabbing his finger on the page. "My dad would've liked this one."

"Check! See, you have one thing off your list already." Amanda giggled with delight. "Now, do you own an internet domain name?"

"No."

"Well, if you decide to use Stotlar Nursery as your name, that's still available, but you need to buy it quick."

"Okay, how do I do that?"

"Laptop?" Bryan led her to the desk in his living room and she took a seat. He hovered over her shoulder as she showed him the site and put the name in his cart.

"Now, all you have to do is put in your credit card information and you will be the proud owner of StotlarNursery.com."

As they traded places so he could complete the purchase, Amanda wandered back to the kitchen table to wait and flipped through her notebook.

"Now you have two things marked off the list. We can do this," she said encouragingly.

"We?" Bryan said as he joined her in the kitchen. "Are you going to stick around and tell me just what I'm supposed to do with that domain I just bought?"

Amanda smiled and patted his shoulder. "I am. I'm going to make you a simple website just to start out that shows your location and hours. Just basic stuff until you're up and going. We will tweak it along the way, but you have to have an internet presence. I'll use this logo you picked out and we will need a nice picture of the place to put on the homepage after you get new signage and the weather improves."

"Is everything on the list this easy?"

"It is. I promise. It's just details you need to clear up to improve the launch of your new business. You'll want to do a grand opening in the spring and get people out here to see what you've got. That will get the ball rolling."

Looking over her shoulder out the front windows she saw what looked like a few flakes of snow.

"I think it's starting to snow. Let me get out of here before it starts coming down. I've got to get home to dinner anyway. I think I've left you with enough to think about for a while." She smiled at his bewildered look. She was rushing him but he needed the help and he could see she was the person to help him.

Amanda hurriedly packed up her notebook and slipped on her coat, barely pausing to say goodbye.

He had been wondering all day how he was going to approach her again. He had so enjoyed her visit Saturday and thought she had too, but he didn't know if she meant for them to be just friends. He didn't want to offend her by assuming more, but he wanted more.

Bryan's head was spinning with concerns on whether he could finance this vision he had. It seemed Amanda had thought more about his business structure than he had although he'd done little else all winter.

A big snow would help his finances as he hadn't gotten as much plow work as usual this winter. That would help bring Amanda's dreams to fruition.

Sheri Richey

Chapter Twenty-One

Conrad answered his ringing phone with hesitation. He always had to steel himself a little to pick up when he knew Bobby Bell was on the other end.

With a heavy sigh and a forced relaxed resolve, he said, "Harris here."

"Connie! So, what happened today? He's out?"

"Yes, Ellis was fined and released."

"I figured as much after I read the report. Your guys didn't have nothin'."

"Do your guys have anything on him? Was he helpful when you questioned him?" Conrad had not been provided any update after the sheriff's visit and could only assume that they didn't get anywhere either.

"Nah, he wouldn't talk. So, do you know where he is? Are your guys watching him?"

Conrad didn't tail released people, and he hadn't ordered anyone to follow him. Knowing Roy though, he had probably tried.

"No, we have the vehicle impounded. He can't claim it without a valid license. Someone picked him up, and he left town. That's all I know."

"Do you have the plates on his ride?"

"I don't but one of my officers might. I can check and get back with you."

"Good," Bobby barked gruffly. "We need to keep an eye on him."

"Will do, Sheriff," Conrad said as Bobby ended the call. Sam Crawford was on dispatch tonight so he sent him a message to find out the tag number and relay the information to the county.

He eased into his jacket and decided to drive down to the Juniper Junction to meet Cora because the snow was starting to accumulate. The Juniper was a local Indian restaurant that he didn't visit often enough so he was pleased with the dinner plans.

He hoped Shawn Ellis was never coming back to Spicetown because he didn't want to call Bobby Bell back again. It was going to be a long four years before the next election.

§

Bryan stirred some soup on the stove and wished he had put something on to cook earlier.

He could have asked her to stay for dinner but the snow would have ruined that. She would have declined because of the fear of driving home.

He could tell by her abrupt reaction to a few flakes that she wasn't going to risk being snowed in at his house. The fantasy enchanted him though.

He was waiting for the phone to ring. Soon he expected he would be called in to plow. The hours weren't good, but it paid well. Not too many people were willing to drive in a blizzard all night. He turned to grab the coffee pot and fill it with water because the night would demand a lot of him.

As he sat down to eat, he looked at all the little pots and remembered the glow around Amanda as she talked of plans for his business. She had big ideas, bigger than his, but she believed in them. Maybe she believed in him, too.

That successful dream she seemed to shine with became his dream, too. He finally felt it was possible to become prosperous. He'd only worried about getting by before, but her confidence in him was infectious and she had made his dreams grow tonight.

Tomorrow he would get his inventory lists together and sketch out some displays. He'd make some calls to get estimates on a new sign and write some ad copy. Then he'd price some new order forms and tags with his imprinted logo. He needed to look and act professional to be treated that way. His father had told him that.

§

Cora was already seated when Conrad arrived. She was right in the middle of the room as usual. She never wanted to miss anyone coming or going. She smiled at him when he came in the door and darted her eyes to the right before looking down. Glancing over, Conrad saw Saucy hunched over a plate at a small table against the wall with his back to the door.

"Evening, Chief," Cora said as Conrad pulled out a chair. "Fancy meeting you here."

"Evening, Mayor. Hope you didn't order this snow. It's going to cost you money." Conrad chuckled as he saw Cora's nose crinkle. She hated the unexpected expense the city incurred when they had to plow the snow. It was one of those expenses she could never estimate accurately. Cora didn't like estimates, she wanted definites.

"I told Jimmy Kole it was his call tonight. I'm not even going to look at it. Whatever I do, it plays games with me. As soon as I call the plows out, it stops. If I don't call, we get a blizzard. I've given up weather forecasting."

Conrad laughed at Cora's bluster and picked up a menu. "Have you said hello to our friend?"

"No," Cora said leaning over and lowering her voice. "I don't think he knows we're here yet."

After they had placed their order, Cora stirred her tea and put away her reading glasses. "Did you by chance speak to the sheriff today?"

"Indeed, I did," Conrad said, surprised by the question.

"I could see the dark cloud around you when you walked in the door," Cora said as Conrad smiled. Cora could read him well.

"It went okay. As usual, he wanted information from me, but didn't want to share anything."

"He's asking about the Ellis boy?"

"Yes, he thinks I should have been tailing him when he was released so he would know where he is. I still don't really know what he's looking for. He doesn't have anything on him, but he suspects him of something. Something that's linked to the firework theft."

"He doesn't want you to get there first."

Conrad nodded, but he didn't think that was the reason. Whatever Bobby was looking for was something happening in Paxton.

"At least Saucy is staying out of trouble. I haven't seen him in a few days," Conrad said glancing over his shoulder where Harvey Salzman was finishing up his meal.

"I haven't seen him either but they are bringing him a check now so I guess we can find out." Conrad watched Cora wiggling her fingers in a subtle wave Saucy's way.

Conrad turned when he saw Cora's smile and also waved at Saucy so he ambled slowly over with his check in his hand.

"Hi, Saucy," Cora said holding her hand open to offer him a chair. "Join us."

"Oh, thank you." Saucy pulled out his wallet as his phone vibrated. "I'd love to but I need to get home before this weather gets worse."

"What have you been up to?" Conrad patted the seat of the chair next to him for further encouragement. "I haven't seen you for a while. Have you been away?"

"Oh, no," Saucy shook his head vigorously as he glanced at his phone. "I've just been out and around like usual. This snow though, I may have to hole up for a bit until it passes. I don't like to be out driving when it's like this. You know people just drive crazy when the weather is bad."

"The plows will take care of it. Everything will be fine," Cora said, trying to keep him talking. "Is your sister doing okay? I haven't seen her in a long time."

"Yeah. Yeah, June is fine. I need to go check on her. I'll tell her you asked after her but I need to get going."

Conrad opened his mouth to try to keep him from running off, but Saucy was too quick. Turning to Cora, he said, "He's nervous as a cat."

"Yes, but he's always that way," Cora said.

"True. I'll drive by his place after we eat and see if he went home."

Chapter Twenty-Two

The snow had been falling daintily when dinner began but by the time Conrad walked out to his car, it was twirling in a cold wet wind that was biting on his skin. He saw Cora waving at the snow plow driver as she got into her car across the street. It looked like Jimmy Kole had made the right call.

He waited for Cora to pull out and quietly followed her home at a distance as he customarily did if she was out at night. They never spoke of it, but he was certain she knew he was back there. Her silence told him that she appreciated him watching out for her.

He circled her block on Basil Boulevard once she was safely in her home and turned to drive slowly towards Sage Street. The roads were showing signs of icing up but his cruiser still moved smoothly.

As he neared the intersection of Sage Street and Dill Seed Drive, he could see a dark panel van in Saucy's driveway and his white truck parked on the street up ahead on the left. He turned a block before the intersection and circled around to approach Saucy's house front on Dill Seed Drive instead, so his headlights shined on Saucy's driveway.

He saw the van doors open towards the garage door which was also raised up. Saucy had his outdoor flood lights on but Conrad couldn't make out who was out there. He'd always wondered what was in that garage, so he pulled his cruiser behind Saucy's truck, blocking the van in the driveway and got out slowly to approach.

Standing in the yard, he paused before approaching to watch the men take boxes from Saucy's garage and load them into the back of the van. He didn't see Saucy around and didn't know either of the two men loading but someone was sitting in the passenger seat of the van.

As soon as he started to take a step forward, Saucy popped out of his side door near the garage and waved while he trotted towards Conrad.

"Hey, Chief! Fancy seeing you twice in one night."

"Do you know these men?" Conrad said softly once Saucy had joined him on the lawn.

"Oh, sure Chief. I just let them use my garage for some storage and they're here to pick up their things. Nothing to worry about."

Conrad felt Saucy met him in the yard to prevent him from moving forward so naturally he advanced another step. He wanted a closer look.

"They'll be out of here in just a minute. Can I offer you some coffee? It's pretty cold out here. Why don't you come in and I'll get you some? I've some already made up."

"No, thank you," Conrad said as he continued to approach the van. Just as he was aligned to the passenger door, he heard the door handle click as the van door opened slightly and the inside light came on.

Conrad's eyes locked with Shawn Ellis' in a silent challenge.

"Saucy, you know this man?"

"Well..." Saucy stammered as Shawn climbed from the van to stand before the Chief.

"He was just helping me out with some temporary storage, Chief. Nothing to worry about." Shawn moved to put his body between Conrad and the back of the van.

"What were you storing, Saucy?" Conrad said to Saucy while not removing his eyes from Shawn.

"Just stuff, Chief. Nothin'..."

"Nothing to worry about," Shawn said finishing the sentence for him. "We had a short-term arrangement. I'm leaving the area now and that's why I'm having my belongings moved."

Conrad walked around Shawn and looked closely at the boxes. He couldn't make the man open the sealed boxes, but he studied their size and looked for labels.

"I think I will take that coffee from you, if you've got some made," Conrad said as he glanced back at Saucy.

"Sure. Sure, Chief. Come on in." Saucy rushed up the steps to hold the door open for Conrad.

Once they were inside, Conrad got out his phone and called Sam at dispatch.

"Sam, I need a plate. George-Adam-Charlie 5743... One more thing, Sam. I'm at Saucy's house. Can you call Bobby and tell him I found what he's looking for? You can let him know where I'm at... Thanks."

It took Sam a few attempts to guess who Bobby was, but Conrad felt confident he understood before he disconnected. Saucy looked shaken by the conversation, but he didn't want to alarm him.

"Gotta let them know where I'm at," Conrad forced a snicker. "Sure as I wander off, someone'll be huntin' me."

"You keep awful long hours, Chief. I'm sure you're a busy man." Saucy handed him a large mug of coffee. "Did you want sugar or milk?"

"No, this is just fine. I appreciate it."

"Always happy to help you out. You have helped me many times."

"Well, maybe you can help me again," Conrad said as he watched out the side door window. "What are you doing with these guys, Saucy? These are not good guys."

"I know you arrested him for driving without a license, but I didn't know he was a bad guy. I just thought he needed my garage for a little while so I tried to help. It wasn't until later after it was all stored that he caught trouble with you. I didn't know he was a bad guy--"

"But how did you get connected to him?" Conrad interrupted Saucy's nervous chatter and tried to look him in the eye. "He didn't just knock on your door and ask to use your garage."

"Well, no," Saucy said as he wiped down his counter avoiding Conrad's glare and concentrated on rubbing a kitchen sponge vigorously over an imaginary stain. "I met him through a friend, just briefly. I just thought I was helping out a friend. That's all."

Before Conrad could ask for the name of the friend he was failing to disclose, he heard the van doors slam shut and felt his phone vibrate in his pocket.

"It looks like they're leaving now. Do you need to go out and talk to them before they go?"

"No, I'm sure they'll just be on their way." Saucy continued tiding up his kitchen.

"Well, you better check your garage and see if your personal items are still there. I hear your new friend has a bad habit," Conrad said as he moved to open the door.

"So, where are you headed, Ellis?" Conrad called out as Shawn opened the passenger door of the van.

"Out of town, Chief. I don't want any trouble."

"I can't say I'm sorry to hear that," Conrad said as Ellis slammed the passenger van door shut and the engine started. Conrad came down the stairs with Saucy on his heels.

Saucy went in his garage and turned on the overhead light to look around while Conrad called Sam again.

"Sam, did you reach the sheriff? They just left in that blue van and they're headed down Sage Street… I'll keep an eye out and let you know."

Sticking his head in the garage, he saw Saucy combing over his tools on his worktable.

"Is everything there?"

"Seems to be, Chief. Probably because you were here. I'm glad you stopped by."

"Do you know where he's going?"

"No, I don't know much of anything about him. He didn't say anything to me. I don't expect I'll be seeing him again."

"That's for the best." Conrad put his phone back in his pocket. "I need to go now. Thanks for the coffee."

"Anytime," Saucy yelled out as Conrad moved swiftly to his cruiser. He wasn't going to tail Ellis, but it was worth his time to circle through town and make sure he didn't see him loitering anywhere. He needed to get the word out to Wink, too. He wanted Ellis to leave tonight.

"Hey, Wink. Where are you?"

"I'm on Spearmint Street."

"Shawn Ellis just left Saucy's house in a blue van with Ohio plates, George-Adam-Charlie 5743. He says he's leaving town, but he's got a load in the back that he packed from Saucy's garage. He says it's his stuff that Saucy was storing for him. If you have any guys on the perimeter of town, let them know."

"You want him stopped?"

"Not unless he's speeding. We don't have cause."

"Okay, I'll let them know. What's Saucy doing messing with that guy?"

"No clue. He said he was helping a friend of Ellis' but he wouldn't tell me who that was." Conrad ended the call. Wink would have everyone's eyes on the exits as he turned to head toward town. He wanted an eye on the retailers with a thief lurking around.

Conrad noticed then that he'd missed a text from Sam, "SO sending car".

Sheri Richey

Chapter Twenty-Three

Conrad drove slowly down Paprika Parkway and turned on Fennel Street. Most of the primary businesses in town faced one of these two streets although smaller stores could be found a block or two off this main drag.

Everything appeared closed down and quiet except for the restaurants. Sesame Subs on Paprika Parkway had some diners and Ole' Thyme Italian still had a full parking lot. There were a few cars still at Juniper Junction and The Barberry Tower, but the Caraway Café and the Fennel Street Bakery were closed up tight.

He decided to drive out a half mile on Fennel Street to check the three bars clustered near the edge of town on the main highway. They would be open and might attract Ellis' crew if they were leaving town to head towards Paxton, but there was no blue van to be found.

He did see a county car sitting in the lot and waved to the deputy. He must be the lookout for Ellis that dispatch mentioned in the text. If he was sitting there, that meant Ellis didn't come this way, so Conrad headed back toward Spicetown.

Approaching the downtown area, Conrad heard Wink on the radio responding to another officer. He was reporting suspicious activity in the alley behind Fennel Street. Wink advised the officer he would check it out.

Conrad pulled his car to the curb in front of Ivy's Oils & Organics and got out of the car. Walking up to the window in the front door, he put his nose against the glass and peered into the back where he could see lights were on and the storage room door standing open.

The officer hadn't said it was Ivy's but Conrad hadn't shaken the apprehensive feeling he'd had the day he saw Ellis first go in there. Denise Ivy must be the mutual friend that Saucy mentioned and if Denise Ivy was Shawn Ellis' friend, his opinion of Denise was greatly diminishing.

Conrad pulled out his phone and called Wink again. He couldn't risk Saucy listening to the scanner and tipping anyone off on their whereabouts. He regretted his feelings of distrust of Saucy, but these recent events put his loyalties in question.

"Wink, I'm out front of Ivy's. I can see activity in the back of the store through the front window."

"Yep, Chief. Me and Tabor are boxing them in the alley. It looks like Ellis' van is unloading at her place. You want to talk to him? He's not going to be leaving right away," Wink said with a smile in his voice.

"No, just check and see if Denise Ivy is there and consenting."

Conrad wasn't going to get caught up in harassment, especially on a case that was tied to Bobby Bell. It was always possible that Denise had agreed to store his boxes for him. If she was there and letting him in her store, there was nothing he could do about poor judgment. Cora had been right. Denise definitely knew Ellis.

Conrad placed his next call to dispatch to let them know where he was and asked them to share that with the Sheriff's Office while he continued to look through the front door waiting for Wink's next update.

Shortly after, the county car pulled up behind his cruiser and he walked down to speak to the deputy. When Wink called back, he stepped away to take his call and walked back to the storefront window.

"Chief, she's there. She says he's dropping off product for her, something she bought from him. Want me to let him go?"

"Yeah, let him out. Which way is he facing?"

"Allspice Street. I'll tail him from there."

Conrad went back to the deputy and told him to turn around and Wink would tail him until the deputy could follow.

Conrad got back in his cruiser and turned on Clove Street to wait for the van to move down the alley and Officer Tabor to follow it. With the alley clear, he pulled in behind Ivy's Oils and saw Denise standing at the back door.

Putting his driver's door window down, he glanced up at Denise Ivy to gauge her demeanor before speaking. He expected her to be afraid of the police involvement but her expression led him to believe she was just irritated at their intrusion.

"Evening, Ms. Ivy." Conrad nodded a greeting. "Sorry to interrupt things but we had to make sure somebody wasn't breaking into your store."

He saw her expression soften and continued. "Do you know Mr. Ellis well?"

"No sir," she said meekly. "I purchased some oils from him. His sister was selling them. She had to go out of business, so he was helping her liquidate."

Conrad suspected the oils were stolen but wasn't convinced that Denise wasn't involved.

"Well, I'll be going now," Conrad said hesitating. "Unless you'd like me to wait around until you lock up. I don't mind."

"No. Thanks, Chief. I'll be fine."

No fear — Conrad noticed again as he drove off down the alley and heard Wink radio that he had handed off his tail to the county. The deputy had his man to follow and Conrad was headed home for the night.

Chapter Twenty-Four

Bryan parked in front of Ivy's Oils & Organics and looked over at his box of plants in the seat next to him. He had spent the morning potting sage, rosemary, thyme, basil and oregano into Amanda's little painted pots and they looked entrancing. He was astonished at how much difference it made in their presentation and he would have never thought to do it.

He wasn't sure Denise would like it though. It might take away from her products instead of accenting them because they were eye-catching. He left the second box on his floorboard and decided to take in only one box first to see what her reaction would be.

He saw Denise through the doorway answering the phone as he held the door open for Miss Violet to leave. She had a small bag in her hand and a tiny pot of thyme. Miss Violet had taught Bryan's fourth grade class at Cinnamon

Elementary but he was certain she didn't remember him. That had been many years ago and Miss Violet had retired before he had graduated high school.

"Thank you." She passed him and glanced into the open box of pots. "Oh, these are delightful. Are these little pots yours?" She held up the one she had just purchased.

"Yes, ma'am."

"If I'd known you were bringing in more, I would have waited. I love these little pots."

"You're welcome to trade it out if you see something in the box you like better," Bryan picked out another pot of thyme and held it up her. It was painted a sky blue with flowers all the way around that looked like they were growing from the base of the pot.

"Oh, I love that. My kitchen is blue. How creative you are," Miss Violet said as she reached for the blue pot.

"Amanda Morgan painted them. If you like that better, you can just put the other in the box and take that one."

"Are you sure you don't mind?" Miss Violet scrutinized Bryan, but he just smiled and shook his head. "Thank you, dear. I think I will then," she said as she placed the plain pot in his box.

Bryan, still holding the door, turned to walk into the store and waited for Denise to finish her phone call.

"Oh, shut up, Harvey. You don't know what you're talking about. These small-town cops are stupid. Just forget about it."

Bryan put his box on her counter and she turned around, slapping her chest in shock. He hadn't meant to startle her.

"I've got to go," Denise said into the phone and hung up without any goodbye.

"Oh my, you scared me to death. I didn't see you come in."

"I'm sorry. I came in when Miss Violet was leaving. I didn't mean to startle you."

"Not a problem." Denise waved her hand to disregard his concern and gazed into the box.

"Wow." She lifted a green pot from the box with bumblebees and flowers painted on the side.

"A friend of mine painted the pots," Bryan said cautiously in hopes she would tell him what she thought.

"They're adorable! I love them." Denise pulled each one out to look them over. "These should really sell—Not that the others aren't. I've sold all except two of those you brought last week." Denise pulled an envelope out from a drawer under the counter and handed it to Bryan.

"I have more in the truck. How many should I leave?"

"Bring them all in," Denise said excitedly. "We'll find a place for them."

§

"You're chipper today." Cora smiled at Amanda as she loaded the copier with paper. "Did you have a good weekend, and I just didn't hear about it yesterday?"

"Actually, I did." Amanda giggled. "I painted all weekend, and I had a good time."

"Painted? I didn't know you could paint."

"Well, not like portraits or anything." Amanda pulled out her office chair to sit. "I painted pictures on little flower pots. Silly, I know but I had a good time. I haven't done any crafting since I came home from college and I forgot how much fun it is."

"You'll have to bring one in the office. I'd love to see them. What are you going to do with them?"

"Well, did you see those little pots with herbs in them that were in Ivy's Oils & Organics?"

"Yes. The one on the counter had a tiny sage plant in it. It was cute. I just rarely cook much anymore but they would make a nice little gift."

"Those are Bryan's."

"Bryan Stotlar?"

"Yes, so I painted some little pots for him just to spruce it up a little. You know he's planning to open in the spring with a full nursery of trees and plants. He's going to do yard landscaping too. It's a big expansion and I'm trying to help with some of the design stuff."

"This is right up your alley. Does this mean you two are a thing? I didn't know you'd been out again."

"We haven't actually been out, really," Amanda said hesitantly but revealed a slight blush. "I just like doing this stuff so I offered to help."

"That's nice. It sounds like you had fun. I'm not very crafty myself. I could barely entertain fifth graders when I needed to and usually their art projects looked better than mine." Cora laughed as she walked back in her office.

"I'll look for them the next time I go down there," Cora yelled out the door after she walked around her desk. Maybe it was time to take a trip down Fennel Street today for lunch. The snow had all been cleared from the streets and walkways, and the sun was shining brightly.

"Oh, Mayor," Amanda called out and Cora looked up to find her in her doorway. "I wanted to let you know I did test those oils you gave me and the new ones are good."

"I expected that." Cora gave a sly smile and a wink.

Sheri Richey

Chapter Twenty-Five

While Conrad was making his morning pot of coffee in his office, Georgia Marks had warned him the Sheriff was on his way over. The message did not come with any explanation. Conrad sat down hard in his chair and took a deep breath to calm the dread he felt creeping over him.

"Connie," the Sheriff bellowed as he walked into Conrad's office hiking up his pants at the waist. "Hate to bother you again but I need an interview room."

"Sure thing, Sheriff," Conrad said. They had no one in holding so Conrad had no idea who he wanted to interview, but he wasn't giving Bobby Bell the satisfaction of making him ask. He knew he had to cooperate, regardless. "We're happy to help."

"Got to pick up one of your locals. You want to send someone along?"

"I'm sure I've got somebody nearby," Conrad said turning to his computer monitor. "Where are you headed?"

"Just a few blocks." Sheriff Bell pointed out the office window. "Going to Ivy's Oils & Organics. She's been doing business with Shawn Ellis. Have you ever talked to her?"

"I have. I've been in the store there and I know she's acquainted with Ellis. That's where he was the first time I saw him in town."

"That must be why he gave up her name so easy. He thought we already knew about her. So, what's her deal?"

"No deal that I'm aware of." Conrad leaned back in his chair. "She's a new business, just getting started. She bought some products from him and he delivered them to her after his release."

Sheriff Bell stepped closer to Conrad's desk. "What kind of product?"

"She said they were oils. His sister had to go out of business and he was trying to offload her stock. He was storing the boxes in Harvey Salzman's garage and after his release, he moved them out. He delivered what she purchased to her as he left town. That's what was going on when your officer came over to escort."

"So, what do you know about this Salzman guy?"

"Law abiding senior citizen, as far as I've ever known. Said he was helping out a friend which I assume was Denise Ivy, the owner."

"I need to talk to him too, then." Bobby sat down and leaned forward with his elbows on his knees. "You pick him up for me?"

"Sure," Conrad said, secretly hoping Saucy was not at home. He hated to see him badgered by the sheriff.

They both rose from their chairs and Conrad went out to dispatch to have Georgia radio Roy Asher to meet the sheriff at Ivy's. He slipped into his coat and went out the back to his car as Bobby led his deputies out the front door to their cars. Bobby still hadn't explained what he thought Shawn Ellis had done specifically, but he had to turn his thoughts to Saucy now.

§

While Cora was out for lunch, Amanda did some internet searches on landscapers and nurseries. She printed several that she liked and looked for patterns in the way they presented their products. She knew Bryan wasn't a website designer, but she thought together they could put up a site to get him started.

She sketched a layout with boxes and notes of what could go in each one. She wanted it to look traditional but original at the same time. This was a small town, and she felt the market wanted practical information more than dazzle. She thought Bryan could write some planting tips and plant care ideas for filler.

As she browsed the image files online looking for something serene and natural for a background, she jumped when she heard someone knock softly on the doorframe.

"Hey," Bryan said softly, peeking his head in the door. "Have you had lunch yet? I was just going to grab a bite and thought you might want to go, too."

"Perfect timing!" Amanda motioned Bryan to come in. "Don't worry. She's at lunch. Come look at some of these and tell me what you think."

Amanda showed him the sites she had copied and explained what she thought would be good for his site. Then she showed him her sketch and looked up when he didn't respond.

"Well, what do you like about these websites? I'm sure you don't want to be changing products out every night, so maybe it would be easiest to just list basic tools and products you carry and then have a place to mention sales."

"I don't know what to say," Bryan stammered. "I don't know how to do any of that. It all looks great, but I don't see how…"

"We can do it. It may not be fancy, but a basic site we can do ourselves," Amanda said confidently. "I know how to do a basic design to make a simple website and I can show you how to update it easily."

"Okay, if you say so," Bryan smiled, not at Amanda's confidence as much as at her including herself in the project. "I trust you."

He realized then that he actually did trust her. She'd gone above and beyond to be helpful to him and he hadn't asked for anything. He still wasn't certain if she was interested in the business or in him.

"Let's walk down to the café." Bryan lifted her coat from the coat tree by the door and held it out for her. "I'll leave my car out front."

§

"Hey, Chief," Saucy said excitedly when he opened the door at Conrad's knock. "What brings you by in the middle of the day? Have you had lunch? Are you hungry? I've got clam chowder in the crock pot and it's hot. I could get you a bowl. It'll warm you up. Come in. Come in."

"No. No thank you." Conrad stepped inside the door when Saucy held it open for him. He could smell the chowder and felt his stomach growl. Bobby's visit had interrupted his lunch plans, but he wanted to get this over quickly so Bobby would be gone.

"I've come by to ask you if you'd go down to the station with me for a few minutes." Conrad saw fear register on Saucy's face as he backed up towards his rocking chair to sit down.

"The sheriff is down there and he'd like to talk to you. I offered to come by and pick you up."

"But... but why would the sheriff want me?" Saucy's face twisted with anguish as he spread his hand out over his heart. "I certainly haven't done anything to worry the sheriff."

"He didn't really say, but I think he just wants to know about your interaction with Shawn Ellis. I don't think it's anything to worry about, Saucy. I think he's just wanting to hear what you know about him."

"Oh, I don't know nothin', Chief. I was just helping out Denise Ivy. You know her store is tiny, and she asked if she could use my garage for a short time. I thought it was her stuff until that night he moved the boxes out. He told me then that most of it was his. I didn't know. I don't even know him."

"I understand, Saucy. I'm sure that's all he wants to know, too. He just wants to talk with you. Maybe get a statement from you. It shouldn't take too long. Can you come with me now?"

Conrad could tell when Saucy's eyes darted away to stare at the corner of the room that he was debating whether to submit. It would be better for him to come in. If Bobby had to come to his house, he'd want to snoop around it and that would cause Saucy additional anxiety.

"Okay, Chief, but I didn't do nothin'. Can't I just give you my statement? I don't even know this new sheriff and I'd rather just tell you. We could do it right now, right here."

"I wish I could, but this is his investigation, not mine. It's up to him. I'll ask him once we get there though. Okay?"

Conrad looked around for his coat and walked back to open the door hoping to encourage Saucy to come with him.

§

"I know business stuff is your kind of thing," Bryan said as he pushed his plate forward. "I really appreciate all your help and advice, but…"

"I'm overwhelming, aren't I?" Amanda looked down at her clasped hands. "I'm sorry. I don't mean to be pushy. You're right. I'm excited for you. Starting a new business sounds like lots of fun and I'm enjoying helping. I don't mean to be so pushy."

"No, I don't mean that at all. You're not pushy. You're great! I just feel bad. There's nothing I can help you with."

"Is that why you invited me to lunch? Is this some kind of…? Are you paying me back? Because if you are, I don't…"

"No. I invited you to lunch because I wanted to see you," Bryan said earnestly. "This is a lunch date. That's all."

"Oh, okay. Well, I mean I didn't know. I'm okay with that." Amanda took a drink of tea and glanced out of the front windows to see police cars parked on Fennell Street.

"What's going on over there?" Amanda pointed out the window at the Spicetown Police car parked behind the County Sheriff's car in front of Ivy's Oils & Organics. Amanda had a sinking feeling when she saw them go into Denise's store. She was afraid Chief Harris had taken action on the information she'd given him about the fake oils.

"Looks like Denise is in the middle of something again," Bryan said as he took the check from the waitress.

"I should probably tell you something," Amanda said sitting back as the waitress picked up her plate. "Especially since you kind of do business with her. I wasn't sure it was a big deal, but maybe it is."

Bryan's brow furrowed. "What?"

"Well, the oils that she sells are marked authentic and pure but they aren't. I tested the ones that the mayor purchased and then I bought a couple myself. They weren't pure, and I told the mayor that. She told the police chief."

"Wow." Bryan glanced again out the window as he saw Denise walked to the police car and got in the back. "You think they're arresting her for that?"

"I don't know. I thought the mayor might ask for a refund of her money. I never thought they'd file charges on her, but Cora was upset when I told her. She doesn't like being cheated."

"There goes that business opportunity." Bryan shrugged his shoulders and put his elbows on the table. "The little stuff I had there didn't amount to much. I was just testing the waters a bit. Getting arrested will probably shut her down."

"You are better off. You don't want to be linked to someone with a bad reputation. You'll be open soon enough and can do it all on your own."

"I wish I had your confidence," Bryan grinned shyly.

"I better get back." Amanda looked at the time on her phone as she wiggled back into her coat.

"We'll walk fast."

Out on the sidewalk, Bryan took her hand in his as if it was a normal thing to do and Amanda skipped a breath. She had meant to say something, but the thought was gone with that breath.

"Why don't you come out to the house for dinner and we'll work on this website design. I'll make dinner and you can tell me how we can make a website."

"You cook?" Amanda shrilled. "Sorry, I don't mean to sound shocked. I'm just visualizing."

"Nothing fancy, but I can do the basics. If you're afraid of my cooking, I'll order a pizza."

"No, I trust you. That sounds great."

"Good. What night is best for you? All my nights are the same," Bryan said smiling. "Unless of course it snows. Then my nights belong to the city of Spicetown."

"How about tomorrow night?" Amanda said as they approached City Hall. "That will give me tonight to get my thoughts together? Do you have a color scheme preference? I was thinking nature-like, but green is just too bland. We need something that makes the plants pop."

"I'll leave that up to you. I don't know what makes plants pop," Bryan chuckled.

Amanda bounced up on her toes and gave Bryan a peck on the cheek. "Thanks for lunch." She smiled as she backed towards the front steps. "I'll see you tomorrow night." Waving, she scurried up the steps to the building and left Bryan standing there with a big grin.

§

Amanda entered her office to find Cora at the copy machine.

"Just what did you have for lunch?" Cora said and wanted to giggle herself at how Amanda looked to be bursting at the seams with glee.

"I went down to the café," Amanda said shaking her arm out of her coat. "Bryan came by and took me to lunch

"Ah," Cora said smiling. "So, you didn't ruin everything like you thought."

"It was just a setback. I did mess things up at first, but things are better now—more comfortable. I was just awkward and nervous then. Anyway, we are working on a new website for him and getting ready for spring. He's expanding everything and I'm helping."

"That sounds like a great project. You'll enjoy that. I'm sure he'll need help with setting up his accounting and everything too. You're a wiz at that as well. Sounds like he picked the right girlfriend at the right time."

"You don't think that's why he asked me out, do you?" Amanda's brow furrowed in doubt.

"Amanda! Of course not. Don't be silly. He didn't even know any of that about you when he asked you out. He's just a very lucky guy." Cora shook her head. The poor girl had confidence problems. "Why would you even think such a thing?"

"Sorry. I don't know. I just haven't dated anyone in a really long time."

"It's like riding a bike," Cora chuckled as she went back to her office and Amanda followed.

"Oh, I forgot to tell you, the sheriff was at Ivy's Oils and they arrested her."

"Arrested her!"

"They put her in the back of the car so I'm assuming so. You don't think it's because of the fake oils, do you?"

"Heavens, no. I wouldn't think so. Conrad hasn't said any more about that. I need to give him a call."

"I hope not. I mean, she shouldn't be cheating people, but jail… I hate to think…"

"Don't worry. I'll see if I can find out." Cora picked up the phone as Amanda walked out and called dispatch. She left a message with Georgia that she would like to talk to the Chief when he was free. She hoped he would stop by before the end of the day.

Sheri Richey

Chapter Twenty-Six

"Harvey is up front in the first interview room whenever you're ready for him," Conrad said as Bobby Bell walked down the hallway. Conrad had left Denise Ivy sitting in the last interview room with one of the deputies. She had her arms crossed over her chest and she looked toward the two-way mirrored window completely ignoring the deputy's questions.

"I'm going to tackle Ms. Ivy first," Bobby said as Conrad passed him in the hall.

"Do you want us to get a statement from Harvey for you?"

"No. No, I think we'll need more than that. I'll get to him as soon as I've had a word with her."

Conrad made some coffee and saw the note that Cora had called. She'd obviously heard about the arrest already. He would fill her in after the sheriff left and that couldn't be soon enough for him.

Taking his coffee with him, Conrad went in the viewing room off the interview room and sat down to watch. He was less concerned with Denise and more interested in exactly why Bobby Bell was after Shawn Ellis.

Denise was not cooperating with Bobby and her remarks were going to escalate if Bobby continued his aggressive pursuit. Bobby Bell had never mastered any techniques to read people because his own arrogance got in the way. Conrad returned to his office when the interview turned into threats and intimidation. Nothing fruitful would come from it.

§

Amanda scurried up the stairs to her room as soon as dinner was over so she could begin her website design. She had tried all day to push it out of her mind while she worked but ideas kept turning over relentlessly as she tried to file the mayor's bills and receipts.

She had decided to use only earth tones and post the items for sale as if they were rows in the garden. She used clip art plants and leaves to decorate the edges and sketched everything out first.

She paused only to think again about how easy their lunch conversation had been. He had almost completely dismissed the arrest of Denise Ivy and continued to concentrate on her. He was so attentive and comfortable to be around that they might have been lifelong friends.

When he had taken her hand as they walked, it had fit perfectly and he hadn't been startled by her boldness at all. He reacted as if she had kissed him on his cheek a thousand times.

Although it was all so new and exciting, it also left her relaxed and content.

Her mother had brought up the arrest at dinner and she had admitted she'd heard about it but didn't tell her about the fake oils. She didn't want that all over town by tomorrow.

§

"She's not talking," Bobby said as he walked into Conrad's office, "but she knows something."

"What involvement do you think she has?" Conrad hated himself for asking but he was tired of the cryptic nature of Bobby's interrogation. He couldn't help him if he didn't know what the sheriff was after.

"She knows Ellis better than she's letting on."

"And what do you think Ellis has done?"

"He's a thief," Bobby exclaimed and threw his hands up in the air as he turned to leave Conrad's office.

Conrad clenched his teeth and tried to slow his breathing. Dealing with Bobby Bell always made his blood pressure rise. Of course, Ellis was a thief. He couldn't help him if Bobby wouldn't share and he never wanted to share information, even when Conrad was partnered with him. He didn't want anyone else to help because it would steal the limelight. The problem with that strategy was Bobby Bell couldn't solve anything on his own.

When Georgia called him to dispatch to answer an officer's questions, he saw Bobby Bell in the room with Saucy and walked over to the viewing room to check on him. Another deputy was seated in the room watching anxiously.

"Hey, Chief."

"Hey, how's it going?" Conrad stood at the window and glanced in, surprised to see Saucy was not nervous, but angry.

"Not getting anywhere," the deputy said. "This old guy probably doesn't know anything anyway."

Conrad had doubts about that. Seeing Saucy hold his own with Bobby's brusque interrogation tactics staggered him. He'd always found Saucy to be very complacent and anxious, never combative, but Bobby did tend to bring the worst out in people.

"Denise didn't help you either?"

"No, Bobby thinks she's Ellis' girlfriend, but she sure doesn't claim him if she is," the deputy chuckled and shook his head. "She's one angry broad."

"Were you guys able to track where he took the van loaded with boxes the night he was released? I know you tailed him out of town."

"He went to one of his friend's house in Paxton and parked it, but the next morning the van was gone. We found it the next day in town, but it was empty."

Conrad looked back through the window when he heard Saucy say he wanted to talk to him.

"Well, everyone here is keeping an eye out for Ellis. We will let you guys know if he comes back."

"Appreciate it, Chief."

Conrad ambled back to his office. Bobby would be coming out soon and he wanted to avoid another conversation. Bobby would never let Saucy talk to anyone else and he would have to let them both go.

He shut his office door and called Cora. It was time to give her an update and get her take on Saucy's reaction. His thoughts were more fully developed when he talked them out with Cora and she knew Saucy much better than he did.

§

"Oh, no. Look at the snow! We're having a blizzard," Amanda huffed in disgust.

Cora had just hung up the phone with Conrad and her mind was whirling on other topics.

"I see that. I'd heard on the radio this morning that we could see several inches of snow today and again tomorrow as the storm moved through to the northeast."

Cora started to say that Amanda shouldn't worry because Jimmy Kole would get the plows out. It was January. This was normal, but then she realized why Amanda was so perturbed by it.

"You know, I have a few old ladies I'd like to go check on. This bad weather is really hard on them and I haven't seen Miss Violet at church since Christmas. I think I'll run out and do that before it gets much worse."

Cora slipped on her coat and saw Amanda texting. The weather must be destroying some plans she had made with Bryan.

"You might get a snow plow ride tonight," Cora said smiling. "It might be an odd date, but not everybody gets to ride in a plow."

Amanda looked up startled but then smiled. "That would be an unusual evening but it kind of sounds like fun. I could make us something to eat."

"And some hot chocolate," Cora added as she slipped on her gloves. "Might be memorable."

"Might be." Amanda beamed and began texting again.

"I might even let you leave early, if it was for a good cause. I mean helping clear snow is a vital city service."

Amanda looked up at Cora with raised eyebrows. "Really? I mean, I know. You're right."

Cora walked out smiling. She could tell Amanda was all a flutter inside. Young love was so heartwarming.

Chapter Twenty-Seven

Violet Hoenigberg getting out of her car under her carport as Cora pulled in behind her. Violet had been her mentor when she had first started teaching and they had remained good friends. Her last name had proven difficult for fourth graders to spell so she had become Miss Violet to everyone. She had retired many years ago, but the bond remained. Cora checked on her occasionally and they chatted at church but she was in her eighties and living alone now.

"Are you coming or going?" Cora called out to her as she got out of her car.

"Hello, Cora Mae," Violet said waving. "No dear, I'm just getting home with some groceries. Didn't want to get trapped without food."

It was a common tactic for half the town to buy out the local grocer every time it snowed. Her pantry stock was probably a little low, too. These ingrained insecurities weren't easily cured.

"Let me help you," Cora said opening Violet's back car door and pulling out her sacks. "I was just popping by to see if you needed anything but I see you beat me to it."

"Oh, now don't worry about me. You better get to the store yourself. The shelves are getting bare. This storm may be a bad one."

Violet held her kitchen door open for Cora as she walked in with the groceries and put them on the table. The cute little potted plant on the counter must be one of Amanda's creations.

"Are you sure you've got everything? Do you need anything? I was worried I hadn't seen you the last few weeks."

"Yes, well the cold mornings were just…" Violet shook her head and took a deep breath. "I couldn't get myself to church. These old bones, you know." Violet chuckled and gave Cora a kiss on the cheek. "You run on to the store now and we'll catch up soon."

"Okay." Cora reached for the doorknob. "You call me if you need anything. Anything at all." She gave Violet her most serious teacher scolding look and then smiled. Violet hated to ask for help.

"I will, honey. I'll be fine."

"Stay warm," Cora said as she pulled the door shut and headed back to her car shielding her eyes from the snow that was now blowing sideways into her face.

Backing out of the driveway, she drove cautiously by Amanda's house down to where Saucy's sister lived. Her car sat outside the garage and taking up most of the driveway, so Cora had to leave her car in the street blocking the drive and trudge up to the front door.

Just as Cora was about to give up and trace her steps back to her car, she heard the front door unlock.

"Hi, June. It's Cora Mae."

"Cora! How are you? What are you doing out in this weather?"

"Just checking on people I haven't seen for a while. It's getting bad out here."

"Come in. Come in, dear. You shouldn't be out in this."

Cora stepped into June's living room carefully to keep her feet on the front door mat and June reached for her coat. She slipped her arms out gingerly to avoid getting snow everywhere and slipped out of her boots, leaving them on the mat.

The house was warm but dimly lit and had a musky smell she remembered associating with her grandmother's house when she had been a child. June had scurried away to the kitchen and was calling out to her to follow. She had just heated water for tea and poured some for Cora without asking.

"Dreadful." June sat the cups at the kitchen table. "This weather is just dreadful. I keep telling Saucy that we need to move south. We're too old for this now."

The kitchen was well lit and warmer. Cora could tell June spent most of her time here as there was a newspaper and mail on the table with a little television perched on the corner of the counter. Her mention of Saucy indicated June was unaware he was at the police station being questioned that afternoon.

"Saucy still gets out and around. I run into him all the time downtown and at restaurants but I haven't seen you in ages." Cora stirred the hot tea.

"He can't cook." June shook her head with a mocking smile. "Won't even try. He has to get out. I feed him on Wednesdays but I told him he needed to learn how to fix a few things because he's not always going to feel like traipsing around town every day in search of a meal. He just won't do it."

"I saw your car is out. It is probably going to get buried in snow. They say we're getting several inches. You might ought to put it in the garage."

"Blast it, I wish I could, but Saucy's got it full of junk. I don't know what all is in there but he had boxes to store last week. I didn't know he was going to take up the whole place though. I'm going to make him clean my car off after the storm." June cackled at that and patted Cora's cold hand. "I'm so glad you stopped by. I don't get out much anymore. Arthritis hurts me bad in the winter and I get Saucy to do my errands for me."

"Well, that's one of the reasons I was stopping. I thought you might need something but if Saucy is shopping for you—"

"I haven't been able to reach him yet. Tried calling earlier, but I left him a message to pick me up a few things I'm low on. When he drops them off I'm going to try to get him to eat a little so he doesn't have to get out tonight. It's not safe to be out in this."

"I went to check on Miss Violet, but she was just getting back from the store herself."

"I'm sure everybody's there. Miss Violet gets around pretty good for her age."

"Yes, she does." June was probably nearing eighty herself. "You mentioned your arthritis, does Saucy have you using essential oils on it? I saw him one day in Ivy's Oils & Organics and he told me the oils help with painful joints."

"Oh, I think that's nonsense. He's just trying to help out little Denise, and she's not worth helping. She's never been there for him. Never been anything but trouble for him." June wrinkled her nose and frowned.

"He knows Denise pretty well then?"

"Well, yeah. She's his step-daughter. Don't you remember Alice?"

"Saucy's wife? Well, I didn't really know her. Bing knew her, but I didn't realize Denise was her daughter. I thought Denise was new to town."

"Naw, she left with Alice, but came back to live here when her grandma died. She's living in her grandma's old house just around the corner from Saucy. She's never been anything but trouble."

"Oh, I didn't realize their connection." The information startled her. Why hadn't Saucy mentioned this?

"Yeah, well he always tries to help her. I don't know why. She's never treated him anything but dirty. She has a smart mouth, that one."

"Well, young people sometimes, you know. Do you ever talk to Alice at all? I don't even know where she's living."

"Nope. Don't care to either. I think she's up north of here somewhere. As far as I know she doesn't bother Saucy with anything. He never mentions her but having Denise around may change that. He said her store's not doing too well so maybe she'll close up and move on soon."

"Well, it's hard to start a new business." Cora took the last sip of her tea. "This weather is hard on businesses too, unless you're the grocery store." Cora chuckled and got up to put her cup near the sink.

"I need to get going before I get snowed in. I've got a few more stops to make but I appreciate the hot drink and conversation."

"Well, I'm glad you stopped. It's been too long, but I know you've got a lot to do." June followed Cora to the door and waited for her to get her coat and boots on again.

"If you see Saucy while you're out running around, tell him to call me," June said as she opened the door. "I don't want him driving around in the dark."

"I'll tell him." Cora opened the screen door and tensed as she lowered her head into the blowing snow. "Take care, June."

She hopped into the footsteps she'd made in the snow on her approach to the door but when she reached June's driveway, she edged around June's car to peer through the garage windows. The garage interior lights were on and June was moving among the boxes with her cell phone in her hand.

June's words were muffled at first, but the tone was angry. Maybe June was leaving Saucy an angry voice mail about the boxes. As June's pacing brought her closer, Cora could clearly hear her.

"I don't care about the snow. Get the unit ready tonight."

Cora hustled as quickly as the snow would allow and jumped into her car. Starting it, she turned on the heat then pulled out her cell phone to call Conrad.

Sheri Richey

Chapter Twenty-Eight

Amanda handed up her bag to Bryan's outstretched arm, then one at a time, lifted up each lidded coffee mug as he secured it all in the cab of the plow. Then she took his hand as he helped her leap up the sideboard of the plow and into the passenger seat.

"I've got hot ham and cheese sandwiches, chips and hot chocolate. It's nothing fancy, but it's still warm. Are you hungry?" Amanda was oddly exhilarated about riding in the plow. Bryan had seemed enthusiastic about it when she'd shared Cora's suggestion and promised to bring her home as soon as she got bored. He had joked that it wasn't as exciting as it looked, but she wasn't along for the scenic challenge. She wanted to spend time with him.

"It smells great. I'm so glad you thought of this because the snow isn't stopping and I probably wouldn't have gotten anything to eat all night."

Bryan picked up a duffel bag that sat between them and tossed it behind his seat. "All I have is protein bars that I keep in here for these long nights. Your dinner is a welcome treat."

Bryan had picked up the truck at the county depot while she had prepared their sandwiches. They had talked on the phone while he waited in line to get his truck loaded with salt. The truck was an older model that the county was going to retire so Cora had crafted a deal for Spicetown to buy the truck and be responsible for their own roads if the county would pay for the gas. Even though the truck had been expensive, it meant the citizens got immediate attention in a storm instead of waiting for the county to do the larger towns first.

The citizens didn't realize it, but Cora had made a huge difference with her deal and the town was now much less paralyzed when snow was heavy.

They ate their sandwiches while Bryan told her all about the truck. It was loud with the diesel engine running and this model didn't have the electronic gadgets that the county trucks had but it did have radio communication so she heard the chatter of the county drivers.

The front end was huge and difficult to turn when cars were parked on the street but Bryan had been driving for the city for several years now so he was comfortable talking and shifting gears without concern.

Amanda found it difficult to take her eyes off the road when they approached a parked or passing car and felt relief only when the encounter was behind them. She would never want to drive a snow plow, but it was fascinating to ride in one.

After an hour of talking non-stop, Bryan drove back to the center of town to clean the main streets again. It was after 5:00 in the evening so everything had closed and almost all the cars were off the street.

"I need to call the PD. Somebody's blocking the alley back there," Bryan said pointing. "I'm supposed to clear the alleys for deliveries. Nobody is supposed to block them."

"What do they do? Do they tow them?"

"I don't really know. It's never happened. Maybe their van broke down and they had to leave it."

"You realize that's right behind Ivy's, don't you?" Amanda lifted an eyebrow when she glanced at Bryan.

"Is she in jail?"

"I don't know what happened. Cora called the Chief, but I left early before she came back so I don't have any update from what we saw at lunch."

"Hey, Sammy," Bryan said into his phone. "I can't plow through the alley off Clove Street because there's a van parked behind Ivy's Oils…. Okay, thanks."

"They're going to send a squad car out to run the license plate and see who owns it. I'm going to circle back around Paprika Parkway to see if they get back to me soon. Except for the alleys, I'm done. Let's hope it doesn't start snowing again."

§

"They just released him," Conrad said when Cora relayed all that she had learned from June. "Sounds like I might need to talk to him, but he's not here."

"I can't believe that Denise is his step-daughter. How did I not know that?"

"Cora, you can't remember everybody. They grow up. They change."

"I'm getting old. I'm getting senile. I used to know everybody in this town and every connection. I always knew the children especially, now I can't… I don't know. I'm frustrated."

"Go home and put your car up. I'll come by and pick you up. We'll go check on Saucy together."

"Good idea." Cora said goodbye and pulled away from June's curb. It was so much easier now that she didn't have to harangue Conrad into including her in things like this.

After Bing had passed away and she had taken over as mayor, Conrad had been very uncomfortable with her involvement in his police work. He had never hesitated to talk to Bing about these things but he was wary of Cora from the start.

She smiled in remembrance of the first few times she had taken information to him that she thought would help him on a case. He had looked at her like a stray dog who was being offered a treat from a stranger. Only after years of sharing and proving her talents, had he comfortably made her a part of his pack.

Now, just when she needed it most, she was losing her connections to the town and its people. She felt a small pang of panic when her memories failed her. Maybe she was getting too old for this job.

§

"They're going to tow it," Bryan said as he ended his phone call. "The mayor told them to."

"Did they tell you the owner's name?"

"No, just said to wait for it to be towed. A tow truck is on the way."

"It's not Denise's, is it?"

"I don't know what she drives."

"Maybe she's in jail and was getting ready to move it when they took her away today."

"Maybe," Bryan said shrugging. "If so, she'll have to bail it out when someone bails her out." Bryan laughed at his own joke but saw Amanda frowning.

"I just hope it isn't over the oils. I feel bad for even telling the Chief about it."

"You didn't do anything wrong," Bryan said squeezing her hand. "You did the right thing. They needed to know.

"Honestly, I don't think it's about the oils. I've overheard her on the phone several times when I've been in the store and she's up to something. She's always whispering and seems angry with whoever is on the other end. A couple of times it was someone named Harvey. Maybe a boyfriend? I don't know, but just…"

"Just what?" Amanda leaned forward.

"Sinister? I don't know. It just didn't seem like normal chatty conversation. It seemed like she was telling someone what to do. Bossing someone or scolding. It just gave me a bad feeling. I wouldn't want to be on the other side of those phone calls."

"Hmm," Amanda said, but it was drowned out by the diesel engine shifting into gear to pull into the alley as the tow truck pulled the van out the other side.

Maybe Denise wasn't a very nice person. Usually good people don't get dragged away from work by the police, but it could happen. Amanda was relieved to know she hadn't hurt an innocent person. Somehow, she felt absolved of any wrong doing by just thinking Denise was a bad person on her own already. It was weirdly comforting.

"Now, I'll take you home," Bryan said as they pulled out of the alley. It was the last street on his route.

"You can come in and have something warm to drink."

"Thank you, but I can't. I have to get the truck back to the county so it can be cleaned. The salt has to be removed right away to keep the plow working right. Your mom and dad probably wouldn't like a late visitor anyway."

"It would be fine. I didn't know you had to clean it. Do you do it?"

"I pull it into a station and dump the salt off the back. There is usually a line from other trucks coming in at the same time. Are we still on for dinner tomorrow night?"

"Sure—Well, if the roads are okay." Amanda wrinkled her forehead. "I mean if it doesn't snow any more."

Bryan stopped the plow in front of her house and she felt his fingertips take her chin gently to turn her head towards him. When their lips touched, she stopped hearing the diesel engine running and the radio chatter. Heat snaked up her neck until she was certain she looked flushed and she skimmed her fingertips across the stubble on his chin until she reached the smoothness of his cheek.

"Thank you for riding shotgun with me tonight and for bringing dinner," Bryan said staying within inches of her lips. "It's the first time I've ever enjoyed plowing snow."

"You're very welcome." Amanda smiled and leaned closer to him. He didn't talk as much as she did, but he always seemed to say the right things.

He kissed her again with a smile on his lips and she took his face with both of her hands to keep him close. When his lips parted against hers, the kiss was passionate but still gentle. It was heartwarming to know there could be passion without aggression. Bryan was everything that her previous boyfriends had not been. He was sweet. Such a simple word but it made all the difference.

Bryan jumped out of the truck and came around to help her down. She knew this first embrace was melting all the snow around them but managed to steal one more kiss before her mother turned on the porch light. Bryan smiled and released his hold on her as he pushed the truck door shut.

"I'll see you tomorrow," he said as she walked to the porch and waved quickly before going inside the house.

Chapter Twenty-Nine

"Good evening, Mayor." Conrad smiled as Cora knocked her boots against the edge of the car's door frame before she got inside the car.

"Dreadful stuff," Cora said slamming the car door shut with a huff. "I guess you heard about the van?"

"I did. I heard dispatch run the plates and called Sammy. He said the van was abandoned behind Ivy's place. Nobody around. Said you told him to tow it."

"I did indeed. There's a sign posted back there that says vehicles cannot block the alleyway. The bakery needs that alley for deliveries every morning and the sign gives me the right to tow."

Conrad nodded as he backed down her driveway. He was grateful she had responded that way.

"The tow gives you the right to search it, doesn't it?"

"Sure does," Conrad said haughtily. "Do you want to make a quick stop before Saucy's? Mike is checking out the van now."

"Yes, let's take a look." Cora fastened her seatbelt for the short ride back to the police department.

Mike waved to them when they pulled in the garage and walked over to Conrad's window as he rolled it down.

"Just getting started, Chief. You want it printed?"

"No, not yet. Is there anything in the back?"

"Not a thing. I just looked."

"Tell you what." Conrad shifted the car into park. "I'd like for you to call county and tell them what we have. Explain the plow and that we've towed it. Have them ask the sheriff if he wants us to print it up or whether he wants to send someone over."

"Will do, Chief." Mike rubbed his arms with his latex gloved hands.

"It's his case and I don't want to step on any toes. Of course, if they tell you to proceed, then go ahead, but I'd rather it be their idea."

"Gotcha," Mike said slipping into his coat. "I'll let you know what they tell me."

"Okay, thanks."

Conrad backed out of the garage quickly so Mike could lower the door from the cold. The garage wasn't heated, and they only had a space heater in the stall to keep warm when they worked.

"That was a good call," Cora said. "I'm anxious to know what might be found in the van, but it wouldn't be worth the backlash if it angered the Sheriff's Department."

"And I don't want the blame if they don't find anything. Bobby throws blame around pretty easy."

"Are you going to tell him about the boxes at June's house? I don't want to see Bobby busting in there and scaring June over it when the boxes may really be Saucy's."

"No, not yet. We don't really know what that's about. I'm hoping Saucy is going to tell us."

Driving up to Saucy's house, they could see the outside flood lights on, but no truck in the driveway. It wasn't unusual to not see lights on at the front of the house when Saucy was home, but his kitchen light on the side wasn't on either. Conrad pulled the car into the driveway, careful to stay in the tire paths made in the snow.

"Wait here and let me see if he's home." Conrad released his seat belt and opened the door.

"It doesn't look like it but it is about dinner time. He might be out getting something to eat." Cora looked at the snow tracks in the headlights.

Cora listened to the windshield wipers flap from side to side and thought about the day they were all in Ivy's Oils & Organics together. Saucy had boasted about all the remedies the essential oils provided right along with Denise's sales pitch, yet he and Denise didn't interact much at all. If Denise was his step-daughter and he had a connection with her that compelled him to help her, why wasn't he sharing his relationship? He had never told them he knew her, and she had addressed him as Mr. Salzman that day. Were they intentionally wanting to keep it a secret? What could be the motivation for that?

When Conrad slid into his seat and closed his car door, Cora saw him staring straight ahead. There were no fresh tire tracks leading into the garage. "He's not home. It doesn't look like he's been home," Conrad said glancing at the snow on his boots.

"No. Maybe we should—"

"Drive by Denise's house?" Conrad interrupted to finish her sentence.

"Yes, we should." Cora nodded as Conrad buckled his seatbelt to back out of the driveway.

Denise lived just around the block on Sage Street and Conrad drove by slowly. Saucy's truck was parked in the street and lights were on in the house but he drove on by.

"It might be a good time to go see June now," Conrad said and looked over for Cora's nod. Maybe June would let him look in the boxes in the garage if she hadn't talked to Saucy yet.

"She seemed annoyed that they were taking up so much room. She said they belonged to Saucy so she might want to ask him first."

"Do you think she's going to let me look in the boxes?"

"I don't know. She might if she thinks they really belong to Denise. She doesn't think highly of her and she feels like Denise treats Saucy poorly. Maybe if you tell her about today, she'll show you just to clear Saucy."

"Let's give it a try. All she can do is say no."

Conrad turned the corner and headed toward June's house. It was only a few blocks away. Pulling up to the curb, Conrad drove into the same ruts that Cora had carved out of the snow earlier that day and they both started the march for the door.

It took June a few minutes to answer, but she seemed delighted at the company.

"Come in. Come in. I just made some hot chocolate and I have a cinnamon Bundt cake fresh baked today. You have to try it."

Cora and Conrad stomped on the doormat to remove the snow from their boots and stripped off their coats while June bustled ahead into the kitchen to get plates.

"Did you see Saucy when you were out and about today?" June plated them each a piece of cake and opened the cabinet for mugs as they sat down. "I made the cake thinking he'd be here for dinner tonight but he hasn't shown up yet."

"Do you need anything from the store? I know you were expecting him to do some shopping for you," Cora said accepting a mug of hot chocolate from June.

"Oh, nothing urgent, I guess. I just thought he'd be around."

"Well, I saw him today," Conrad said tapping a napkin on his mouth. "The cake is delicious, June."

"Yes, it's very good," Cora said. "I told the Chief about our visit today. He saw Saucy down at the police department earlier."

"What was he complaining about this time?" June laughed with a rasping cough. "He's always got it out for somebody."

"Well, no. This time it was different. The sheriff wanted to talk to him."

"What? Really? I sure didn't know that. What could the sheriff want with him? I can't imagine Saucy could help out Sheriff Bell."

"Well, I wasn't in there when they talked, but the sheriff talked to Denise, too."

"Oh, no. Denise has probably gotten him tangled up in some of her foolishness then. That girl has never been anything but trouble to him."

"Cora tells me that Saucy stored some boxes in your garage recently," Conrad said as June took the empty plate from him and put it in her sink.

"Yes, that's why my darn car is out there stuck in the snow. Not that I use it much, but you know, you want to be able to use it if you need it."

"Of course. I think I can probably get someone over here to clear off your car and driveway, if that will help you," Conrad said as June took Cora's plate to the counter.

"Oh, I don't want to trouble nobody," June said dismissively. "I don't need to get out for the next few days anyway."

"Well, I hate to see you stuck out there."

"If I need to go somewhere, I'll just get Saucy to take me. It's his fault anyway." June smiled as she sat back down at the table.

"June," Cora said softly. "Do you know what's in those boxes out in your garage? I mean, have you looked in any of them?"

"Why, no. Why?"

"Well, I just wondered if the stuff really belonged to Saucy.

"Whose stuff would it be? You think he's storing stuff for Denise in my garage?" June's voice escalated slightly and tension built in the room.

"We don't know that," Conrad said calmly. "I just know he had boxes in his own garage recently and they weren't his belongings. At least he said they weren't. He said they belonged to a friend."

"Psst, Saucy don't have any friends," June said with a flippant wave. "Even if he did, he wouldn't give them his garage. You think the stuff in my garage came from his?"

"It's possible," Conrad raised his eyebrows and nodded. "And it may not belong to him."

June slapped her hand on the table. "If he put that fool girl's stuff in there and let my car get covered in snow, he's going to hear about it."

"I don't want to make you angry at Saucy, now," Conrad said soothingly. "I just wondered if you'd looked in those boxes and knew what was out there."

"No, I hadn't given it a thought."

"Would you like me to take a look?" As Conrad offered the help, Cora hoped she'd welcome the assistance.

"Oh, no. Thank you, but I'll just talk to Saucy about it when he gets here." June rose from her chair.

"Is it something I could move over for you?" Conrad got up from the table and walked into the utility room off the kitchen to peer through the window to the attached garage. "If I moved some things over, we might get your car in there."

June followed him through her kitchen and into the utility room where her washer and dryer were neatly stored on one side. Boxes of various sizes were stacked three or four high in the garage. One box had markings on the side indicating it originally held a television, but the others were smaller.

"Did Saucy recently get a new TV?" Cora asked June, looking over June's shoulder to the garage. "I see a TV box out there. Maybe he reused the box."

"No, he ain't had anything new in years except that truck. He don't care about household type things one bit. He listens to the radio or the scanner more than TV anyway. He's always trying to do your job, isn't he, Chief?"

June chuckled at her joke. "Can I get you both some more hot chocolate? There's plenty." June tried to lead them back to the kitchen, but Cora waited hoping June would open the door. Conrad wouldn't want things to be construed later than he had violated any property.

"You know, I think I can stack them a little better and move things around," Conrad said with his hand on the door knob.

"I think there's just too many of them," June said but she didn't stop him from opening the door.

When she saw they were all taped, June turned to go back into the utility room and came out with scissors in her hand to open the boxes and handed them to Conrad.

"Go ahead, Chief. Let's see what's in there. Here, let's open this little one right here." June tapped on the small box just outside the utility room door.

Conrad opened the scissors and used one side to slice open the tape of the closest box. It was fairly small and unmarked but when they pulled back the flaps and peered in, they saw smaller boxes. June picked up the small white box and opened it.

"Candles. I guess Saucy's not worried about the power going out. Maybe this is Denise's stuff, and he just didn't tell me. He knew I'd say no if he asked me to store stuff for her."

June tossed them back in the box and took the scissors from Conrad's hand as Conrad walked a little farther into the maze of boxes and saw one large box with the flap not taped. As June wandered back into the house with Cora, he flipped up the edge and got a quick glance before following the ladies into the house.

As they walked into the kitchen, Cora heard her phone chirp that a text had been received and she slid her hand into her purse as she continued to nod at June while she complained about the loss of her garage.

"I believe there are storage units available just south of town. You could always tell Saucy that he needs to move these boxes there so you can store your car properly for the winter." Conrad reached into his shirt pocket to retrieve his vibrating phone.

Glancing at the message, he tapped a quick message and looked at Cora.

"I'm sorry for the disturbance tonight, June, but I've got to get back to the station right now. I thank you for the warm drink and cake though. It was a real treat."

"Oh, Chief, it was my pleasure. I'm always glad for a little company. Cora, you're welcome to stay a spell and visit."

"I'm sorry, June. Maybe another time. I really have to get going, too. I'll surely check back in on you though real soon."

"Well, all right," June said as she ambled slowly to the front closet to help them retrieve their coats.

"I'm telling Saucy in the morning to clean up my car and vacate my garage," June said sharply. "I'm not having any more of this nonsense with Denise and I wish he'd stop getting involved with her. She's nothing but trouble."

Cora gave June a hug, and they said their goodbyes as she let them out the front door. When Conrad heard the front door click shut, he looked back at Cora.

"Bobby has pulled Bryan Stotlar in for questioning and wants to interview him at the PD."

"I know. Amanda just texted me. She's at the PD and she's frantic. She was talking to Bryan on the phone while he waited at the county shed to get the plow cleaned when the deputies showed up. Is Bobby trying to tie Bryan to Shawn Ellis? What's going on?"

"I don't know but we need to go down there and find out. Bobby needs to tell me what he's up to."

Cora fastened her seatbelt as Conrad walked around and got into the driver's seat. "Doesn't Bobby know you're on the same team?"

"No, and frankly, I don't want to be on his team."

"Well, I know," Cora said as Conrad started the car, "but law enforcement should be sharing information."

"Yes, but he has never done that. Even when we were partners, he wouldn't tell me what he was up to."

"You were partners? I didn't know that."

"Briefly, yes. We didn't make a very good team then either, but I don't know anyone that was very successful working as a partner with Bobby."

"What happened?"

"Well, years ago, we were forced to work together but Bobby wouldn't even tell me when we were assigned a new case. He would go out and try to work it alone first. When I would find out about it, I'd go do my own investigation. Bobby couldn't work with anyone else but he could sure take credit for someone else's work."

"He was your partner, but he wouldn't work cases with you?"

"The first time it happened, it caught me off guard. I watched him accept congratulations from the squad for a job well done and even brag about it when he had done nothing.

"The second time it happened, I confronted Bobby about it. That was a pretty unpleasant exchange, and we ended our partnership over it. I asked to be reassigned and Bobby was left to work alone. His success rate was zero, but at least he wasn't ruining anyone else's career."

"Have you ever talked about it with him?" Cora asked. "I mean, does he ever mention it?"

"No, we didn't speak for years. Even when we saw each other in the office, we didn't make eye contact. I never even told anybody but Bobby wasn't as kind. He tried to slander my name whenever an opportunity arose. I thought I saw the last of him when I left the sheriff's office."

"I guess the chance of ever getting an apology is zero." Cora shook her head in disgust. "Now you're stuck with him again."

"These recent election results were hard to swallow," Conrad admitted. He realized from the ache in his jaws that his teeth had been clinched throughout every encounter and now he was headed into another.

"Right now, I just want to help Bobby get the information he needs so he'll leave. He can have all the credit for it he wants."

They parked near the employee's side entrance to the police department and scampered in the door. Sheriff Bell was pacing around the dispatch area with his hands tucked in the back waistband of his jeans massaging his lower back. Amanda was sitting in a plastic chair in the hallway and her eyes widened when she saw Cora enter the room. Conrad walked to the viewing window and saw Bryan in an interview room with a deputy.

"Sheriff," Conrad nodded. "Can I talk with you for a minute?"

Cora walked directly up to Bobby Bell and tipped her chin up. "Sheriff, I would like to speak to my administrative assistant that is sitting in the hall. Is that all right with you?"

Conrad's shoulders straightened from the tension in the room. Bobby didn't realize it, but Cora was seconds away from laying right into him if he didn't respond the way she wanted. She had an edge to her voice he learned quickly after spending time around her. A polite impatience that was curt and direct. One wrong move and the teacher in her came out to reduce him to a naughty schoolboy caught in the wrong place at the wrong time.

"Mayor! Certainly." Bobby waved his arm to invite her to walk by him. As Conrad turned toward his office back down the hallway, Sam peered at him from the dispatch booth with apprehension, but Conrad turned as Bobby shuffled behind him.

§

Cora reached out to touch Amanda's arm when she saw her red eyes and Amanda embraced her in a trembling hug.

"I'm so glad you're here. Thank you for coming so fast. I didn't know what to do when he told me on the phone that they were taking him in. He didn't even know why."

"It's going to be all right," Cora said rubbing Amanda's back. "The Chief will get this all straightened out. I'm sure it's nothing."

"I know it's about Denise Ivy. I could hear them say her name over the phone before it disconnected. Bryan hardly even knows Denise. He just sells those little plants—"

"I know, Mandy. It's going to be okay. The Chief will explain everything to the sheriff. I'm sure the sheriff is just trying to learn more about Denise and Shawn Ellis."

"But Bryan doesn't know anything," Amanda sniffed.

"Well, he's been around them and he may know something that could help them. I don't think they're after him for anything. It's just questions. He has a case to work."

"If they aren't after him, then why couldn't they just call and ask him?" Amanda's teary trembling was turning to rage. "He would have answered their questions. You don't just pull somebody out of a snowplow in front of everybody and make it look like you're arresting him if you just want some information."

"I agree," Cora conceded. "It does seem a bit rash, but the sheriff has his way--."

"Of being a bully," Amanda blurted out. "He told the dispatcher to put Bryan's little girlfriend out in the hallway when I came in here asking questions. So condescending," Amanda huffed and pulled her coat down.

The anger was straightening Amanda's spine and Cora wanted her weepiness to turn to strength. If this was more than just Bobby's brusque manner, Bryan would need her to be supportive, not sappy.

"Let me go see what I can find out," Cora said. "I'll be right back."

§

"Come in. Have a seat," Conrad said gesturing Bobby to a chair as he shut the door.

"I have some information that might interest you." Conrad sat down at his desk. "I'd like first to know why you are questioning Bryan Stotlar."

"He's just part of the picture," Bobby said grasping his ankle and pulling it up over his knee. "He knows Ellis and that Ivy lady."

"What do you have on Ellis?" Conrad thought he knew, but he wanted to make Bobby talk.

"I think he's good for some burglaries in Paxton. He didn't do them alone though."

"What was stolen?" Conrad glared at Bobby Bell as he fidgeted in his chair and put his foot back down on the floor. "Specifically, what goods have you recovered or had reported stolen?" Conrad added to fill the silence.

"Different things," Bobby said shrugging. "Retail theft, mostly."

"Specifically," Conrad said again. "What goods have been reported? What retail?"

"A whole slew of places," Bobby said throwing his hands up in the air. "A book store, a gift shop, a small appliance store and a pawn shop."

Conrad stared at Bobby for several seconds and waited in the silence until Bobby's eyes rose to meet his. "Do you think Ellis stole your fireworks?"

"It's possible." Bobby nodded and jutted his chin up in the air. "He's a thief. It could have been lots of things. I just need to get someone to roll on him so I can recover the goods and charge him."

"Well," Conrad said rolling his shoulders to relax. "I can tell you that Bryan Stotlar isn't involved."

"Oh, you know that, do you?" Bobby tilted his head in a sneer.

"I'm pretty confident about it," Conrad said with a satisfied smirk as he shifted his weight in his chair. "I can also tell you where your fireworks are."

Just as Bobby opened his mouth, there was a light tap on his office door.

"Come in," Conrad called out, ignoring Bobby as he sat up abruptly.

"Chief," Cora said softly. "I'm sorry to interrupt you both, but I'd like to take these kids home if that's okay with you." Cora looked from Conrad to Bobby and smiled sweetly. "It's getting late."

Bobby looked uncertainly at Conrad and Conrad nodded briskly. "I'm sure that would be okay. Isn't it, Sheriff?"

"Well," Bobby frowned.

"If you need anything more from them, I know where to find them," Conrad reassured him and Bobby nodded.

"Okay. Okay, yeah."

"Thank you, both." Cora backed out of the door and closed it softly.

"Now what are you up to?" Bobby growled at Conrad.

"Let's take a ride." Conrad stood from his desk and waited for Bobby to stand, too.

Sheri Richey

Chapter Thirty

Cora waited patiently while Sheriff Bell ordered his deputy to release Bryan and then he walked down the hallway following Conrad without speaking a word to her.

Cora stood to see Bryan walk out in the hallway and embrace Amanda as she clutched to him with teary eyes. There were definitely feelings there. She could see it in both of them and it left an ache of emptiness in her heart.

Shaking off selfish feelings, she walked out into the hallway and asked them if they would take her home. Conrad had picked her up, and she didn't have a car at the station.

"Thank you so much, Cora," Amanda said grasping her arm. "I was scared to death when the deputies showed up while we were talking on the phone. I didn't know what to do. I just ran down here."

"I didn't do a thing," Cora said patting her hand. "It's all going to be all right. They just had to cover all their bases, but I know it can be scary."

They walked out to the parking lot to Amanda's SUV and Bryan opened the passenger door for Cora. It took her a few tries but with Amanda pulling on her hands she finally was able to hoist herself into the seat.

"So, they just told you that you could go?" Amanda asked Bryan turning to the backseat.

"Yeah," Bryan said shrugging. "The deputy said they would let me know if they had any more questions but that I could go for now."

"What were their questions?" Cora asked leaning forward.

"They wanted to know how I knew Denise, how I met her and what our relationship was now.

"I told them that I just introduced myself a few months after she opened and showed her my plants. I asked her if she would be interested in putting them in her shop."

"I was afraid of all this," Amanda said. "After I found out her products weren't good, I was afraid it would be bad to do business with her but I never thought it would mean getting questioned by the police. This doesn't have anything to do with the oils, does it?"

"No, I don't think so," Cora said shaking her head. She didn't feel like she could share much yet but she didn't want Amanda to feel that she had caused the police trouble.

"They didn't mention that to me," Bryan said. "They just wanted to know what I knew about her, about her personally, and I really don't know anything."

"Well, you said once that you thought she had a boyfriend," Amanda said. "Remember? She was yelling at him on the phone."

"Oh, yeah. I forgot about that. Some guy named Harvey and I don't know if he was a boyfriend but she wasn't very happy with him. I didn't think to tell the police that."

"I think it's best that you just put this all behind you," Cora said. "You haven't done anything to worry about and I don't think they'll need to talk to you again."

"You know something." Amanda crinkled her eyes and smiled at Cora. "I understand if you can't tell me, but I can tell that you know something."

Cora chuckled as they pulled up to her house and turned into the driveway.

"I'll see you tomorrow," Cora said to Amanda. "Thank you for the ride, dear. You drive safely."

Bryan started to get out of the car to help Cora to the door but she waved off his assistance and stomped her boots on the front mat.

Once she was in the house and she saw the light on, Amanda backed out of the driveway slowly. "Do you think I should call the sheriff and tell him about the boyfriend?"

"No. You've basically done that already by telling Cora. The information will get there if it's important to the case. She has an inside track."

§

"Sorry, it's so late, Miss June," Conrad said as June answered the door with a shocked expression on her face. "And I'm sorry to bother you right at the dinner hour, but do you think we can come in?"

"Certainly, Chief," June said as she backed into her living room and reached for his coat.

"This is Sheriff Bell," Conrad said as June draped their coats over an arm chair by the door. "If you don't mind too much, I'd like to show him what you have in the garage."

Bobby nodded his head and smiled at June. Conrad was pleased Bobby was abiding by his instruction to stay quiet and not alarm June. His usual brusque approach to everything would have either scared or angered her. Conrad offered his assistance on a conditional basis. He wasn't going to help Bobby get inside if he refused to cooperate.

"Of course, Chief," June said wringing her hands nervously.

"I think it might help him with something he's working on so I wanted to show it to him."

"Okay. Of course, I want to help. Shouldn't I call Saucy first?"

"I'm going to visit him next, so I'll let him know," Conrad said nodding decisively.

"I don't know what help it will be, but you can come through my kitchen here."

June reluctantly opened the door and picked up the scissors that were still sitting on the washing machine as they walked through the door.

"Ma'am," Bobby held his hands up. "Can you give me those scissors?"

"What? Oh, these?" June looked down at the scissors in her hand and hesitated. "Sure. Here you go." June thrust them at Bobby and laughed. "I wasn't going to get you with them. I thought you'd want to use them to open the boxes."

Conrad smiled as Bobby took the scissors and relaxed.

"I want you to know that stuff out there isn't my brother's. I thought it was but when we opened it earlier, I knew those things didn't belong to him."

Bobby followed Conrad to the large box that he had peered in earlier and Bobby nodded discreetly.

"Ma'am, would you mind if I had some fellows come over and move this stuff out for you? I think I might know who it belongs to."

"That's exactly what I'd like you to do," June exclaimed. "You can load it all up and dump it at Denise Ivy's house. That's where it all belongs."

"My guys will get it all cleared out for you," Bobby said warmly.

"Will they clean off my car too? It's all covered with snow because that stuff is taking up all my space."

"I think we can arrange that," Bobby said smiling at Conrad. "Let me make a call."

Conrad patted June on the shoulder and led her back inside where it was warm while Bobby called his office.

"You were right all along, Miss June. Those boxes don't belong in there and I think Sheriff Bell will take good care of it for you."

"Well, I'll be glad to see it gone, but I hope Saucy doesn't get mad with me. I don't want to see him in any trouble."

"I'll explain everything when I go by there. I'm going to leave Sheriff Bell here with you."

"That'll be fine," June said as Conrad stepped back into the garage and arranged things with Bobby. The sheriff had called his office and had deputies coming with a van to collect the boxes.

Conrad slipped into his coat as he went out the front door and pulled his phone from his pocket.

"Bobby is all taken care of. I'm going to talk to Saucy now."

"I'm ready. Pick me up. I am watching out the front window for you."

Saucy would be more forthcoming if Cora were there. She had known him all her life and Saucy had a lot of respect for her. Lifetime citizens of Spicetown still viewed Conrad as a newcomer sometimes, despite the decade he'd lived there.

Conrad called dispatch and told Sam he was leaving the sheriff at June's house and to send whoever was available on patrol over to June's to coordinate the transfer of the garage contents while he waited on Cora to make her way to the car. She was shuffling down the snow shoveled steps before Conrad came to a stop in the drive.

"I'm so glad you drive a normal car," Cora said as she plopped down and reached to pull the car door shut. "I thought I'd never get up in that SUV of Amanda's."

"You should have told Sam to get you a ride. Somebody on patrol could have run you home." Cora was spry for her age but she was not much more than five feet tall and he had to chuckle. Her remark gave him a vivid memory of trying to get her out of a boat and onto the dock one day when he went fishing with her late husband, Bing.

"Oh, I hated to be a bother. So, how did it go with Bobby? How was June?"

"Bobby was the perfect gentleman," Conrad said straightening his shoulders as he drove.

"You coached him a little then?"

"I did. He didn't like it much, but he behaved."

"So, June is okay with it?"

"Yes. She was worried that Saucy might be mad, but I told her I was going over there.

"Bobby isn't going to come after Saucy, is he?"

"I don't think so. He really wants Ellis."

"He's short-sighted," Cora said huffing. "Ellis isn't running things."

- 257 -

"You don't think so?" Conrad grinned but Cora didn't notice. He had been thinking the same thing.

"I don't. Saucy is involved, but he's not running it either. Bryan told me that he heard Denise yelling at Saucy on the phone when he was in the store. Saucy is afraid of her for some reason."

"So, you think it's Denise? You're just mad because she sold you fake oils," Conrad said chuckling at Cora's blustery expression. The thought did give him pause though.

"Maybe, but I think June knows more than she's saying. We need Saucy to spill it," Cora said as they pulled in the driveway. The lights were on in the home and it appeared Saucy was there. "You can be the good cop this time."

Conrad tossed his head back as his eyes rolled up. Cora was in detective mode now and she could get feisty when she felt wronged.

"You are not the bad cop." Conrad stopped the car in front of Saucy's garage. "You are the mayor; don't forget."

It was Cora's turn to roll her eyes as she jerked the car door open. The outside lights came on and Saucy was at the side door before Conrad could reach Cora at the door.

"Saucy, we need to talk to you," Cora said before Saucy had a chance to greet them. "Can we come in?"

Saucy opened his screen door and Cora charged in, not looking back to see if Conrad was keeping up.

"Evening, Saucy. Sorry for the late hour, but can we talk to you?" Conrad said while Cora took off her coat.

"Sure, Chief. Is anything wrong?"

"Well, I need to tell you about my evening," Conrad said as Saucy guided them to the living room and Cora sat down.

"Okay." Saucy stared at both of them solemnly from his chair across from the sofa. Conrad was surprised at his demure reaction. Saucy always offered drinks and rattled on about a dozen different things which made it difficult to get a word in when you had something to say.

"I went to see June tonight..." Conrad began.

"Is she okay?"

"Yes, she's fine." Conrad nodded as he noted some anxiety flutter Saucy's breathing. "I took the sheriff by there, too."

Conrad paused expecting Saucy to dive in with a jumble of questions but he said nothing. Cora always grew impatient with Conrad's gradual approach and had to jump in.

"Do you know why?" she asked Saucy pointedly. "Do you know why they visited June tonight?"

"No." Saucy widened his eyes with fake innocence. "Did she call you? I should have stopped by there tonight but it was so late."

Conrad glanced at Cora with a warning in his eyes. She wanted to pounce on Saucy but he didn't think it was time for that yet.

"Saucy, the items June has stored in her garage, the boxes... Are those your boxes?"

Saucy looked down at the floor between them and said nothing. Cora moved to the edge of the sofa where her feet could touch the floor, but Conrad held out his arm to slow her.

"Were those the same boxes that you had in your garage?" Conrad kept probing for a question that Saucy would answer.

"Yes, Chief," Saucy said slowly and took a deep breath. "They aren't my boxes."

"Do you know what's in them?"

"No, Chief. I don't have any idea."

"Who do the boxes belong to?"

Saucy held his head in his hands and looked down at the floor. "June told me to stay out of it. She just wanted them stored."

"Who told you?"

Saucy wouldn't meet Cora's eyes and she may think she was playing bad cop, but Conrad knew he was about to see the school teacher come out in her. "The items in those boxes were dangerous. Did you know that? Did you know they could have hurt somebody?"

"I was just trying to help," Saucy said innocently. "She needed a place to put some things."

"Look—" Cora snapped, and Conrad again tried to calm her with a look.

"Saucy, we know Denise was your step-daughter," Conrad said glancing at Cora. "What we don't understand is why you are keeping that a secret."

Saucy looked at the floor again, searching for words or a story to fabricate, Conrad didn't know which, but Cora's patience was up.

"Harvey Salzman." Cora rose to her feet. "You look me in the eye right now and tell me what's going on. What is Denise mixed up in and why are you involving yourself in this nonsense?"

"I don't know anything about it," Saucy pleaded. "I was just trying to help."

"Since when do you do something you don't want to do? I've known you for fifty years and you don't just let people walk all over you. Now, what's with this girl? Why is she dictating what you do?" Cora was speaking louder than necessary but Saucy's behavior was frustrating her.

"Saucy." Conrad breathed in calmly trying to diminish the tension. "We can go ask Denise if you prefer. We know what she's done and what your involvement has been. We want to understand why you did it. That's all."

Conrad didn't really know what Denise had done, but he thought Denise was the one telling Saucy what to do.

Saucy slumped in his chair. "Denise is, was my step-daughter and she, well she is hard to handle. She scares me sometimes. I don't really know anything, but I felt like I had to help. I didn't know what was in there, but I thought the stuff might be stolen."

Cora lowered herself back to the sofa and relaxed.

"June is having a hard time. Denise, too." Saucy said shaking his head and still looking at the floor. "I didn't know how to help."

"June?" Conrad said and glanced at Cora.

"I've tried to help out but I don't have much. They were working on something but I'm not really included. I don't know anything."

"So, they have Ellis stealing things for them? And you were helping out, too?" Cora started to stand up again when Saucy didn't respond but Conrad put his hand on her arm.

Saucy lifted his head and met their eyes. "Denise said she would tell you that I am a child molester, that I molested her when she was little. She threatened to file charges on me and tell you horrible things about me." Saucy covered his face with both hands.

"I never did those things, I never, but she is so mean and I knew she would do it. I couldn't take that. I couldn't have you think that. June couldn't stop her. She wanted me to stay out of it. Just store some boxes and butt out. I tried to talk to them. I tried to tell them there was another way."

Conrad saw the pained expression in Cora's eyes as Saucy began to sob into his open hands.

"Tell us what you know," Conrad said.

They all sat in silence until Saucy had calmed, blown his nose, and offered them refreshments. Cora pulled a leather folder from her oversized satchel she called a purse and handed it to Conrad as they moved to the kitchen table.

Cora was quiet as Conrad peacefully extracted all the facts that were known to Saucy and helped him complete his signed statement.

Saucy shared his limited knowledge of Denise coordinating burglaries for June with Shawn Ellis and helping him sell the merchandise they collected. Denise had started out an honest business person, but when money became tight, she looked for alternative ways to keep her business open. She came to Aunt June for help and was following her lead. That meant using Shawn Ellis to do her dirty work.

Cora was stricken with the tortured look in Saucy's eyes as he recounted the way Denise had treated him since she had returned to Spicetown. Her earlier suspicions that Denise was the mastermind did not encompass the level of evil this elder abuse had caused. Now knowing that his sister was behind it all, she saw Saucy's spirit was broken and he was ashamed.

As they left Saucy's house, Cora hugged him and patted his back. She told him she was sorry this had happened to him and tried to reassure him that they didn't think badly of him at all. Standing in his doorway waving goodbye to them, he appeared a smaller man for the experience. She worried about leaving him alone as they rode to her house in silence.

"Come in," Cora said as she turned to open the car door when they arrived at her house.

"I have to make some calls."

"I know. You can do that while I make us something to eat."

Conrad nodded and turned off the car to follow Cora into her house. She went directly to the kitchen and Conrad slipped into her living room and called Sheriff Bell for what he hoped would be the last time that night.

After dinner Cora nestled herself into her favorite chair in the living room, propped her feet up on the ottoman and tossed the chenille cover over her legs as Conrad sat in what would always be Bing's chair. Her cat jumped in Conrad's lap and rubbed her head against his chest just as she had always done to Bing.

While Cora had boiled some pasta for a quick dinner, Conrad had talked with the sheriff by phone and had one of his officers drop by to pick up Saucy's statement. Once the sheriff received the information, June was arrested, and an arrest warrant was issued for Denise. They would both be taken to Paxton that night.

Conrad felt Saucy was cleared, and the stolen merchandise was no longer in his town.

"I have good news and bad," Conrad said as he stroked Cora's orange cat, Marmalade.

"I could use some good right about now."

"Well, Darren Hudson tells me that he has a friend in the sheriff's department who's working on this case. They went to state police training together. He can find out what's going on and keep me in the loop because you know Bobby isn't going to talk to me."

"How soon can we expect to hear something?"

"That's the bad news. It's going to take a week to get forensics back most likely. They took prints off the van and they're doing the same on the boxes and contents. I just hope they can hold on to Ellis with something else until those results come in.

"Bobby never would tell me what he had, but he had to have some evidence of Ellis doing those burglaries to start him on this trail. Denise and June could be cleared unless Ellis talks. I don't know that there is any real evidence against June."

"What a day." Cora shook her head in disbelief.

"Indeed, it was," Conrad said, but there was relief that the niggling feeling was gone.

"Do you think Ellis will talk now? If he's just a gopher in the plan, I would think he would want to sing. No reason to take all the blame."

"I expect Denise will try to implicate him when she gives her statement," Conrad said. "June will probably try to implicate Denise. The problem is that we know Denise and Ellis have a connection. We don't have anything to tie June to all this except statements from people involved. That's not going to be enough for a conviction."

"Bobby will probably fall for that because he wants Ellis," Cora sneered. "They all need to be held accountable."

"I'm sure Ellis is involved. He probably did the thefts. I think Denise is the one telling him when and what to do. Behind all of that is June. That part surprised me."

"It broke my heart to see Saucy tonight," Cora said with her hand over her heart. "He can be an annoying little man, but he has a good heart and he wouldn't hurt anyone. I'm sure he didn't know how dangerous those boxes were. He would never have stored them if he had known they contained fireworks."

Conrad smiled. Cora was a unique mixture of soft and strong. She had been angry with Saucy earlier that night but Conrad knew she only wanted the best for him. She was protective of her people and Harvey Salzman was one of her people. June had betrayed them all.

Conrad glanced at his phone when it vibrated with a text message. "Denise is on her way to county jail tonight."

"Good riddance!" Cora shuffled her feet under the blanket. "You know, there seems to always be problems when we let new people into town. Can't you do something to stop that?"

Cora laughed at her own joke and shifted in her chair. "If you're going to live in Spicetown, you have to follow the law."

"Oh, they know that and they try." Conrad smiled at her sarcasm. "The rumor is they're all afraid of the bad cop mayor."

∞∞∞

Sheri Richey

★ The Spicetown Star ★

Store Owner Arrested

--- Denise A. Ivy, 32, was arrested Saturday night by Paxton County Sheriff Robert Bell on charges of felony theft and possession of stolen merchandise.

Ivy is suspected of leading a five-person theft ring involving multiple retail burglaries in Paxton that occurred from late November through early January.

Ivy is the owner/operator of Ivy's Oils & Organics on Fennel Street in Spicetown, Ohio. She is currently being held on bond awaiting trial.

Also arrested and charged were Shawn Ellis, 36, of Paxton; Arnold Thomas, 38, of Red River; and William Parks of Paxton. June Tully, 74, of Spicetown was arrested and released.

TONIGHT	TUE	WED
21° LO	27° HI	29° HI
Plenty of clouds	20° LO A p.m. t-storm in the area	20° LO A p.m. t-storm in the area

STOTLAR NURSERY
Your Garden
HEADQUARTERS
OPENING MARCH 1

Sheri Richey

Next in The Spicetown Mystery Series

A Bell in the Garden

I'd love to hear from you!

Find me on Facebook, Goodreads, Twitter, my website or join my email list for upcoming news!

www.SheriRichey.com

Sheri Richey

Printed in Great Britain
by Amazon